THE EPIC TALES OF A Misfit HERO

THE EPIC TALES OF A Misfit HERO

MATT PETERSON

BONNEVILLE BOOKS,
AN IMPRINT OF CEDAR FORT, INC.
SPRINGVILLE, UTAH

ISBN 13: 978-1-59955-999-5

Published by Bonneville Books, an imprint of Cedar Fort, Inc.
2373 W. 700 S., Springville, UT, 84663
Distributed by Cedar Fort, Inc., www.cedarfort.com

LIBRARY OF CONGRESS CATALOGING-IN-PUBLICATION DATA
Peterson, Matt, 1977- author.
The epic tales of a misfit hero / Matt Peterson.
pages cm
Summary: A coming-of-age story about Andrew, a member of the Church of Jesus Christ of Latter-day Saints, who is the newest deacon in his quorum.
ISBN 978-1-59955-999-5 (alk. paper)
1. Aaronic Priesthood (Mormon Church)--Juvenile fiction. 2. American fiction--21st century. [1. Aaronic Priesthood (Mormon Church)--Fiction. 2. Mormons--Fiction. 3. Conduct of life--Fiction 4. Interpersonal relations--Fiction. 5. Church of Jesus Christ of Latter-day Saints--Fiction.] I. Title.

PZ7.P445165Epi 2012
[Fic]--dc23

2012015542

Cover illustration by Neil Robinson
Cover design by Angela D. Olsen
Cover design © 2012 by Lyle Mortimer
Edited and typeset by Melissa J. Caldwell

Printed in the United States of America

10 9 8 7 6 5 4 3 2 1

Printed on acid-free paper

For Melody,
who never stops believing in me

Contents

1. Deacon's Collar 1

2. Folding Underwear 7

3. Unexpected Prayer. 10

4. "Mr. _____ " 12

5. Face-Plant for Beehives 16

6. This Is *Not* Disneyland 22

7. Pink Poncho 25

8. Decoy 30

9. PG Words 35

10. Weak and Simple 41

11. Mosquito's Bite 47

12. The Accident 52

13. Panic. 56

14. Prayer .61

15. In a "Crunch" 64

16. On the Move 68

17. High Ground 72

18. Sausages 75

19. A Five-Advil Situation 79

20. Nobody Notices a Deacon 85

21. "Welcme" Home 90

About the Author 96

Deacon's Collar

Have you ever noticed the little piece of a dark necktie that hangs below the collar of a deacon's white shirt? They call it "Deacon's Collar," and I hadn't really noticed it until the first time I sat in the front row with my new quorum before church. We all had it.

When you turn twelve, you can get other things too. For example, I got a camping backpack, a couple of wrinkle-free white shirts, a birthday party (with the same birthday hats we've used since I was seven), and an interview with the bishop to receive the priesthood.

But Deacon's Collar is universal. *Every* twelve-year-old Latter-day Saint boy seems to get it. It's a symbol of graduation from Primary and an official end to the pine-wood derby years.

"Andrew, make sure to hold the tray in your right hand," Curt whispered loudly. He was sitting on the bench a few spots down from me. "My brother said that was the most important part," he added without even looking up.

According to Curt, his brother was a member of a bishopric and on the verge of becoming a General Authority. I found out later that he was really just an assistant ward clerk in Ohio or Kentucky or someplace where he was attending dental school. I guess it's okay to look up to your older brother, but Curt made his brother out to be a cross between Batman and Brigham Young.

"*Brother Green* told me that being *reverent* was the most important part," I spat back. Curt glanced over at me and shrugged as if to say "your loss." He settled back into his seat and opened his scriptures on his lap. I didn't need Curt's bossy attitude right now. This was my first time passing the sacrament, and I didn't want to mess it up.

I looked at the rest of the boys on the bench. What a sight. There was JD, a wiry, blond-haired boy who always wore untied tennis shoes to church. He sat playing with a Band-Aid that was at least a week old on his thumb. Next to him was Curt, who looked a lot like JD but with actual church shoes on. He was scanning the podium to see if anyone was watching him "read" his scriptures. Mason sat on the far side—his brown hair uncombed, mouth wide open, and eyes pasted shut. When you're around Mason, it always seems like it's a Saturday morning and you should still be in bed. On my other side was Ryan, the tallest of our group, with dark hair and an ironed shirt. He was trying to follow along with the opening hymn but was on the wrong page. Last on the bench was Doug, a little red-headed guy wearing his dad's tie, which was about a foot too long for him. He was the oldest of us all, and he sat leaning forward with his forearms acting as tent poles between his chin and knees.

This was the deacons quorum of the Highland Fourth Ward. Not really something you're going to see depicted in one of those church paintings anytime soon.

After the hymn, Bishop Christiansen called someone to be Relief Society Weekday Special Musical Number and Quilting Coordinator (or something like that), and he introduced a couple of eight-year-olds that got baptized on Saturday. "As you know," he continued, "the Scouts will be leaving on a backpacking trip this Tuesday. We would appreciate your prayers on their behalf."

Strange. The last time I heard the bishop ask for the ward's prayers was when Jake Burlow left to serve in the army in Afghanistan. I can understand the extra concern for a guy who's going to get shot at every day, but I wondered why he would make that request for a bunch of twelve-year-olds going out into the woods for less than a week.

Bishop paused for a second to look down at us and raised his eyebrows briefly. The expression almost implied that he didn't expect us to come back. I sort of felt like one of those guys in the movies who has to defuse a bomb or throw a magic ring into a lava-filled mountain. I could picture the scene as we left: sobbing mothers waving white handkerchiefs as their sons hiked off to meet with destiny—fathers choking back tears as they grabbed the young heroes by the shoulders to say good-bye. But maybe this was all just my imagination.

I couldn't dwell on our impending doom because it was time to pass the sacrament. I was definitely nervous for this, but not sweaty-palms-and-armpits nervous. I had been studying the way the deacons pass the sacrament every Sunday of my life (except for a two-month stint at age six when I was really into coloring). I knew their routes, their positioning, and their demeanor. Now it was *my* time to perform.

The priests finished the blessing, and I followed the line to receive the trays. So far, so good—I hadn't messed up yet. As I walked back to my assigned route in the hard-chair section, I noticed my mom and dad smiling at me. Mom was blotting her eyes with a Kleenex, like I wouldn't be able to tell that she was crying. Dad looked happy to see me fulfilling my first priesthood duty, but I could tell he was sweating uncomfortably in his suit. He kept eyeing the AC control two rows in front of him. (Sister Rollins had no idea that so many people were silently willing her to press the "on" button of the thermostat.)

The rest of my family wasn't paying attention to me at all. My older sister, Kari, was reading the *New Era*, probably looking for pictures of "cute" boys in other stakes throughout the world. Mom says that kind of behavior is "all part of being a fifteen-year-old girl," but I don't get it. I'm pretty sure you aren't supposed to cut out pictures of strangers in Church magazines and hang them up in your locker.

My younger sister, Paige, was helping Jacob clean up Cheerios he had probably already spilled three or four times. Paige is everybody's favorite, including mine. She is ten years old, and while not yet as pretty as Kari, she is just as popular. She could even make friends with the jerks in detention—but she would never be in detention, because, well, carving her initials into a desk or pushing someone off the monkey bars isn't exactly her style.

Jacob is three years old and the youngest in our family. Maybe one day he will look up to me in the same way Curt looks up to his brother (but hopefully without the made-up stories about Church service).

Anyway, I was able to perform my duty in the overflow with no embarrassment. I didn't drop a tray, miss a row, or sneeze up a bunch of phlegm. It sounds crazy, but I've seen it happen—and it's definitely my worst fear. Tyson Harding will never live down the time three or four years ago when he sneezed at least a pint of the really nasty stuff into his hand while passing the sacrament. He walked around with his hand in his pocket for the rest of the ordeal and, according to legend, made at least two Laurels throw up.

The only time that I felt a little uncomfortable was when I handed the tray to Becky, my next-door neighbor since we were both five. She looked up at me and tried to wink, but she ended up inadvertently closing both eyes as if sending a Morse code message via her eyelids. I gave her a semismile, and she blushed as she quickly passed the tray along. The whole exchange was pretty awkward. I don't know why everything seems weird around girls all the time now, especially one I've known forever. But I guess that's another thing that comes along with being twelve. Oh yeah, and acne.

When I returned to my family, I got the old five-second back scratch from Mom and a pat on the knee from Dad. I nestled into my seat and put my head back on the bench. Success. Dad had undone his tie a little to relieve some pressure, Paige was now sitting down watching the speaker, Kari was still reading the *New Era*, and Jacob was about to spill his Cheerios again. Kari didn't even look up from her magazine to dish out the news. "Your fly is down, by the way."

"What?" I looked down, and, sure enough, my fly was completely wide open. I hurried to zip it up and said a silent prayer of gratitude that I had a clean batch of underwear this morning and didn't have to wear my old Transformers underoos—the red ones. But if I don't return from this campout (and apparently that's a real possibility, judging by Bishop's prayer request), everyone will remember me as the kid who forgot to XYZ before he passed the sacrament.

I sighed and reached back to try to fix my collar so that my tie wouldn't show. No luck.

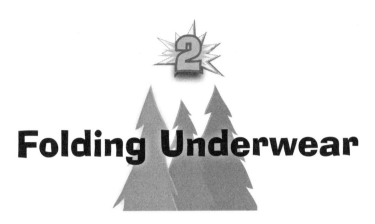

Folding Underwear

Mom, what's our insurance carrier's name?" School had ended a few weeks ago, yet I was still filling out paperwork. Typical. This time, though, it was a permission slip for summer camp.

"I already filled out your permission slip, sweetie. It's on the counter," came the reply from the laundry room. I thought that being twelve meant more responsibility, but Mom had already done my assignment and was doing my laundry as we spoke. It's hard to feel grown-up when your mom is folding your underwear down the hall.

I was excited for summer camp, though; it would be my first extended time away from home. We were headed up to the mountains as a deacons quorum. I guess there was an embarrassing incident at the "regular" Boy Scout camp last summer involving the archery range, the camp director's dog, and two deacons from our ward. (I had to piece the story together from fragments of rumors I heard, but I think I have a good grasp of the episode.) As a result, Brother Green decided to take a year off from Camp Pinewood and put on a ward-sponsored camp. He said that we could go back to Pinewood next summer, but he wanted us to experience backpacking in the wilderness this time.

Honestly, I was happy to avoid the Boy Scout summer camp. I'd heard horror stories of overzealous junior staff chasing you out of the dining hall for having your shirt untucked or for wearing white socks. I could take that from an adult, but not some fifteen-year-old with seven merit badges and an attitude.

More important, I wanted to avoid skits. Nobody really enjoys performing in skits. I had to be in one at a camporee last fall, and I felt like I was seven years old. Only I never had to do anything so silly when I was *actually* seven, so that was weird. I think adults make you do skits to maintain control over you—who would disobey a leader when he has a video of you pretending to be a wheel on a bus or a news reporter or something? Anyway, I was glad to avoid camp this year.

I put the permission slip into the front pocket of my new backpack and scrolled down the checklist one more time: sleeping bag, pad, tent, clothes, flashlight, hydration bladder, camp stove, mess kit. They never put "pillow" on those lists of what to bring, but on the few campouts I had been on, a pillow had been the only thing that helped me get any sleep.

I went to my room to get my pillow but realized that I needed it for tonight. I looked across the room to Jacob's bed; he was sitting in the closet, putting together a puzzle. His pillow was soft and half the size of mine—it would be perfect for backpacking. "Hey, JJ, do you think I could borrow your pillow for my camping trip?"

He looked up from his puzzle at me, then over to his bed. "Foh the Boy Scouts?" he asked. He would probably give away a kidney just to be associated with Boy Scouts. It had taken Mom a few days to convince him that he couldn't go on the campout with me.

"Yep, for the Boy Scouts. And as a trade, you can sleep in my bed with me tonight, okay?" This was my standard payment for any favor I asked of him, but he never got sick of it. His eyes lit up, and in three steps he was already jumping into my bed. He began pulling back the covers to snuggle in.

"After family night, buddy. Not yet!" I laughed. He pouted and pulled himself out of the bed and back to his puzzle. "I'll take good care of your pillow, I promise." He looked at me as if to say "you better," and I grabbed it off his bed. I took it and brought it downstairs to my backpack. It fit perfectly in the side compartment next to my sweatshirt, and I took my pack over to the foyer just as Dad called out that it was time for family night.

Unexpected Prayer

I was the last one to arrive in the living room for family home evening and was disappointed to see that Paige and Kari sat on the old love seat that we got from my grandma. It is pretty much the ugliest couch I have ever seen (it has split-pea-soup-green and mustard-yellow stripes), but it is by far the most comfortable seat in the house. Since it was taken, I pulled out a few throw pillows and found a spot on the floor.

Jacob was conducting, and with Mom whispering in his ear, he welcomed us to family night. "We will sing 'Wevwently, Quietly,' and Kawi will play the piano." He tried his hardest to be reverent and proper during his announcements. He takes conducting seriously, which is pretty much the only thing he takes seriously.

"Then Andwu will say the pwa-oh." He sat back down, forcing himself not to smile while Mom gave him a kiss on the cheek. The rest of family night went as usual—we had a lesson from Mom, scripture reading from Dad, and a closing song. And what happened next caught me a little off guard.

While Kari was saying the closing prayer, she paused for a moment and asked Heavenly Father to bless me while I was on my camping trip. She then asked for His "angels to keep watch" over me. I had heard people talk about the protection of angels before; this was not new. It was new, however, for my big sister to be sincerely praying for her "obnoxious" (according to what she always tells her friends on the phone, anyway) little brother. I felt warmth inside my bones, and for the first time I can remember, I felt a deep love for my sister. Maybe she wasn't all about boys, shopping, and volleyball after all—and who would have guessed that she was actually listening to Bishop in church? Somehow I knew that Heavenly Father heard her prayer and that He was waiting to send His angels to be by my side.

"Thanks, Kari. For the prayer," I said just as I was in the kitchen trying to swallow a mouthful of Paige's chocolate chip cookies. It was as affectionate as I could get.

"You're welcome." She smiled at me. "Just don't forget to leave your stuff outside when you get home so it doesn't stink up the house."

"All right." I laughed back. She was actually joking around with me! "I'll—"

"I'm *serious*, Andy. I hate it when the whole house smells like campfires and BO."

I could tell from her tone that she wasn't joking and that our "moment" was officially over. She grabbed another cookie and turned back toward the family room, probably to check Facebook.

"Mr. _____"

Morning came pretty quickly—the sun peeked through the curtains well before I was ready to get up. I somehow willed myself out of bed and stumbled into the bathroom, where Mom had left a note on the mirror that said, "Don't forget to pack your toothbrush," with a smiley face at the bottom. Again, my responsibility and grown-upedness were being questioned. I'm glad she wrote the note, though, because I seriously would have forgotten. I imagine a few days in the woods with no toothbrush can produce some pretty nasty breath.

I threw some water on my face and quickly ran my wet hands through my hair—just enough to smooth out the bed-head bumps. I almost forgot my toothbrush after all, but I grabbed it and what was left of my toothpaste on the way out. It had been years since I shared toothpaste with the girls, ever since they pleaded their case to Mom that it just wasn't working out. Since then, I've always had my own tube to use as I please.

Downstairs, Mom had put a bunch of cream cheese containers on the table and was toasting some bagels. "Good morning, Mr. Camper!" I don't know how she manages to pull off being so cheery at 6:00 a.m., but she does. *Every* day.

"Hey, Mom." I wasn't going to attempt any clever reply at this hour, although the "Mr. Camper" label deserved some kind of smart-aleck remark. I sat down and started spreading some strawberry cream cheese on a plain bagel.

"Did you remember to pack your too—"

I cut her off before she could finish. "*Yes*, I packed my toothbrush . . . thanks to your note." As I finished, I could tell that she was smiling, even though she wasn't facing me. I really was grateful. Some kids in school barely ever see their moms. My mom is the best, even if she does use silly phrases like "Mr. Camper." I said it again, just so she knew I wasn't being sarcastic this time. "Thanks."

Dad came in from getting the paper and gave me a tap on the head with the sports section. "How's Mr. Backpacker?" Can't anyone be creative anymore? I told him that I was excited as I polished off the last of my slightly over-toasted bagel. Everyone else would be in bed for at least another hour, so I knew that Mom was making these bagels just for Dad and me. Even if they were slightly over-toasted, they were still my favorite breakfast. And Mom knew that.

"We better hit the road if we want to get to the church on time," Dad said as he scanned the baseball standings. It didn't really matter if we were on time or not, though, because I knew that half of the boys would be late . . . as usual. I've grown up with these guys, and most of them rarely ever heard the opening prayer at Cub Scout pack meetings.

I put my paper plate in the trash and took one last drink of milk before tossing my cup in the sink. I hurried up the stairs to get my backpack and the Angels hat I got last year on our family vacation to California. I took the steps two at a time back to the kitchen and realized that I may have appeared a bit too eager. Mom and Dad both smiled at me while I tried to recover and act as unexcited as I could.

Mom gave me a big hug and a few minutes' worth of customary phrases like "I'll miss you," "Have fun," and "Don't forget to wear sunscreen." This was followed by another three minutes of picture taking in our front yard (I'm sure she started her blog entry before we even backed out of the driveway). As I sat in the front seat of Dad's old Honda, I tried to shake off the kindergarten-style farewell and focus on being a twelve-year-old. I was trying to remember if I packed a poncho when I realized that Dad was asking me a question.

"Are you nervous?" I was a little surprised by the question. My dad is normally not one for unnecessary conversation, so I knew that he was really interested in my answer. I flipped the visor down to avoid the orange spotlight that was slowly rising over the horizon.

"A little." It was not exactly the truth—I was nervous about several things: the long hikes, cooking my own food, getting along with Curt, and going number two in the forest, just to name a few. Dad seemed to know that "a little" really meant "a lot," but he didn't let on.

"You'll do great, Andy. I'm really proud of you." Those words couldn't have been more reassuring. It was like he had written them out ahead of time and, after several edits, came up with the perfect thing to say. For one, Dad hadn't called me Andy since I was eight or nine. It reminded me of playing catch in the backyard—it had been way too long since we'd done that.

The other thing that stood out was that Dad was proud of me. For what? Getting all Bs last year in school? For only fighting with my sisters every *other* day? I always thought I was kind of a disappointment to him and Mom. Not the tattoo/piercings/heavy metal kind of disappointment but the "I know he could do better" kind. I could tell that he meant what he said, though. This was starting to be way too much like a kindergarten send-off, so I fought back any signs of tears.

"Thanks, Dad." It wasn't enough, just like it wasn't enough when I said it to Mom at breakfast, but it was all I could think to say. I quickly added, "We'll have to play catch when I get back."

He did a double take, although he tried to disguise it as looking in the rearview mirror. "Awesome," was all he said. He smiled the rest of the way to the church. I did too.

Face-Plant
for Beehives

The scene at the church parking lot was just what
I expected: empty. Other than an old white Suburban
with rusty, bent-up running boards, there wasn't anything (or anyone) in sight. As we pulled closer, I noticed
Brother Green stretched out underneath the hood of his
Suburban, his feet dangling just a few inches above the
ground. This couldn't be a good sign. We'd had at least
a half dozen family vacations interrupted because of car
problems, but we never had issues *before* we left.

Dad parked next to the old Suburban and hopped
out of the car. "Good morning, Aaron. What seems to
be the problem?" I was silently and eternally grateful
that he didn't call my deacons quorum advisor "Mr.
Mechanic."

"Oh, hey, Brother Jensen. Everything is great! I was
just checking the fluids." As he hopped down to the
ground, he hit his head really hard on the hood. I've seen
guys lose it in times like this, but he didn't even say a *fake*

swear word, let alone one of the bombs you hear at school all the time. He just reached back with one hand to cradle his head and stretched his other hand out to greet me.

"You ready for this, Andrew?" His grimace gradually turned to a smile as he gave me a hybrid high five/handshake.

"I think so." I thought he would rip my arm off he was so excited. He wasn't much taller than most of us, and I'm pretty sure Ryan could take him in a game of one-on-one on the basketball court. But his energy made up for being short.

"It's gonna be awesome. I'm so glad you're here," he said, still rubbing the back of his head. I smiled as he let go of my hand and bounced around to the back of our car. He took the backpack from my dad just as he was pulling it out of the trunk. In a flash, he was already jogging over to put it on the luggage rack on top of the Suburban. I guess I wasn't the *only* one who looked a little overeager for the trip.

Everyone else started arriving within a few minutes. Parents said their good-byes and hurried off to work or to get back to their other kids. Brother Green and Brother Campbell were busy shaking hands, collecting permission slips, and loading backpacks. JD, Mason, Ryan, Doug, and I were in the parking lot, playing soccer with a walnut-sized rock when a blue minivan came squealing in. It was Sister Allred, the Beehive advisor, and she wasn't alone.

Four girls piled out of the minivan, most still in their pajamas. We stood there, frozen in a state of terror. What was this all about? Before we could get too carried away in our fears, Sister Allred shouted, "I'm glad you guys haven't left yet. We brought some treats for you!"

I glanced at Doug to see what reaction would be appropriate. He simply said "sweet," and walked right over to the flock of Beehives. The rest of us followed his lead, although with much less confidence.

But on the way across the parking lot, the unthinkable happened. Ryan began walking a little too quickly. Maybe it was the sight of candy bars or thirteen-year-old girls, or maybe it was just nervous energy. But right before he got to the girls, he turned to see if we were still with him. "This is awesome," he mouthed, eyebrows raised. And just as he turned back around, his foot plowed right into one of the concrete dividers that separate the parking spaces.

Ryan's body fell to the ground as if gravity were an older brother pushing extra hard just to be mean. His outstretched hands saved his face from a nasty nose-plant into the gravelly pavement. As he fell, his pocketknife flew out of his pants and skidded across the asphalt until it came to rest at the feet of Katie Norton. Ryan just lay there, facedown, probably trying to convince himself that this was all just a horrible nightmare.

Katie picked up the knife and walked over to Ryan. She squatted down next to him and touched his shoulder. "Are you okay, Ryan?" He nodded his head without looking up. "We made these for your trip." She placed the knife and a candy bar taped to an index card next to Ryan's hidden face. Ryan slowly rotated his head to look at her offering and forced out a muffled "thank you."

The rest of us were too embarrassed for Ryan to say anything to him. Maybe it was better if we just pretended it didn't happen. After what seemed like five minutes of awkward silence, the other girls reluctantly came over with a candy bar and note for each of us. This was undoubtedly the work of Sister Allred.

Becky was still looking down at Ryan as she made her way over to me. She was wearing gray pajama pants and an elementary school T-shirt—the one from fourth grade with an eagle driving a school bus. Her black-rimmed glasses and ponytail somehow made her seem much older. She stood in front of me, and her entire face lit up in a smile.

"Wow," she whispered, now more somber as she glanced back at the disaster scene. "Poor Ryan."

"I guess it could have been worse. I don't really know how, but it probably could have been worse." We stifled our laughter together. Becky handed me a handwritten card taped to a Nestle Crunch. It said: *Remember to pray when you're in a CRUNCH.* There was a little hand-drawn heart next to Becky's signature on the bottom.

I stared at it a little too long, trying to figure out what it meant (the heart, not the cheesy thing about prayer). "Thanks, this will be great for the drive." I'm sure I was blushing now, and I was starting to think that maybe Ryan was the lucky one—at least nobody could see his face.

"You're welcome! I can't wait to hear all about your trip." We made eye contact just long enough to make everything even more uncomfortable. Thankfully, she finally turned her head to look around the parking lot. "Where's Curt?"

"He's not here yet." I looked around too, annoyed that Curt was late once again.

"Could you give this to him?" She handed me another index card. This one had an Almond Joy taped to it. It read: *enJOY your campout.* I felt even more annoyed with Curt now. I was about to say something mean when I noticed that Curt's paper was signed by Becky, but it didn't have the little heart on it. Interesting. Plus, it was a candy bar that nobody really liked, so I decided to bite my tongue.

The other girls were already loading in the van, and Sister Allred was patting Ryan on the back to say good-bye.

I looked back at Becky. "I'll give it to him. You better go—see you later." I think she may have noticed that I was comparing the two cards, and now *she* was blushing.

"Be safe!" she said as she turned to run to the van. And the minivan full of girls was gone just as quickly as it had arrived.

Curt finally pulled into the parking lot, and Brother Green closed the hood of the Suburban. "Let's go, boys. It's time!" I walked over to where Ryan was sitting on the pavement and reached down to help him up from his misery. His hands were bloody, but he couldn't stop looking at the card from Katie.

"You all right, man?" He looked like he was in kind of a daze.

"Perfect," he said as he walked with me back to the

Suburban. JD was already recounting the story to Curt and had to cut it short when he saw us. Ryan buckled himself into his seat and finally looked up from Katie's card. For a minute, I thought he was going to cry. Then, without any warning at all, he started laughing. The infection spread quickly. Soon all of us were laughing uncontrollably, and it didn't stop until we were miles down the highway.

This Is
Not Disneyland

The raindrops started dive-bombing our windshield just as we pulled off the main highway. Typical. Don't get me wrong—I love the rain. When you have to run laps in PE during 120-degree weather, you learn to appreciate a little rain now and then. But it seems like *every* time I go camping, it rains. Not just sprinkles either. End-of-the-world, Noah-type rain that makes your shirt stick to your skin and your shoes feel like a couple of those stringy mops they have at the school cafeteria. I *hate* rain-camping.

The Suburban grumbled over the rough dirt road, which was quickly turning into a soupy mess. Brother Green was telling Brother Campbell about last year's Scout camp fiasco, but I couldn't make out any of the names or details. Brother Campbell just kept looking back at us (at no one in particular) and shaking his head. He was smiling, but I could tell he was quietly wondering what he'd gotten himself into.

He'd only been the assistant scoutmaster for two months, so he was just about as new to the deacons quorum as I was. All I knew about Brother Campbell was that he had only been married for a few months and just recently moved into the ward. Well, I guess I don't really know how long he's been married, but I've seen him holding hands with his wife at church, and he'd called her twice since we left that morning. It's a pretty sure bet that he's a newlywed.

The rain didn't stop for the entire hour and a half it took us to slide down the muddy road to the trailhead. Brother Green put the Suburban in park and leaned over the steering wheel to take in the scene. Apparently every other Scout troop had checked the weather, because ours was the only car in the small parking lot.

I can imagine how it all goes down for those rich, fancy troops. Some scoutmaster rides in on a motorcycle and gathers everyone around. "Well, boys, it looks like it might rain. How about we go to Disneyland, instead?" Applause. High fives. Chartered bus. Hotel. Unlimited churros. And a group picture in front of the Matterhorn with their Class A's on—just to prove it was a Scout trip. Ugh.

But here *we* are, about to hike five miles in a hurricane. Brother Green suggested we say a prayer to see if the rain would let up a bit. He asked Doug to call on someone to say it, and the rest of us naturally stared at the floor to avoid eye contact. "Andrew." It wasn't even a request—he just blurted out my name as he folded his arms and closed his eyes. I guess it was up to me.

I mustered all of my faith and said the prayer, asking for the rain to stop so we could make it safely to our campsite. When I said "amen," I was half-expecting to open my eyes to bright sunshine and a rainbow. No such luck. Almost instantly, the rain seemed to get even louder on the windshield. Everyone looked at me with disappointed eyes.

Luckily, Brother Green jumped in to break the tension. "Hey, guys, no big deal. We're not afraid of getting a little wet, are we? There's no lightning . . ." And then he hesitated just a second too long. "We'll be just fine."

With that, he opened the door and bolted for the trailer. Brother Campbell, like a dutiful assistant, followed his lead. Within minutes, we were all huddled under a giant blue spruce, getting ready to hit the trail. And those cocky rich kids were probably just getting loaded onto the roller coaster at Space Mountain.

Pink Poncho

s that your sister's poncho, JD?" A chorus of laughter broke the long silence. We had all been thinking the same thing, but Doug said it out loud. JD looked down at his bright-pink rain cover and shrugged.

"It was the first one I found this morning, and I didn't have much time." It was just like JD to not care about what he was wearing. It was even more like him to wait until the morning of a weeklong hike to pack up. "At least it's keeping me dry."

I'm not really sure what he meant by "dry." We had been hiking for about two hours in steady, pounding rain. My shoes were soaked through to the point of making squeaking noises with every step, and my fingertips looked like ghost-white raisins. All my poncho did was keep my torso less wet than the rest of me. I was grateful for my new backpack, though, because it had a built-in rain cover that would (I hoped) see to it that I had a pair of warm socks to slip into tonight.

We marched in a single-file line, closely packed together like a train. From engine to caboose we probably only took up five yards. Other than the brief laughter enjoyed at JD's expense, the only human sound was our heavy breathing. The trail was easy to find—mostly because the rain somehow managed to gather right where our feet were supposed to go. We ended up walking just to the side of the newly formed (and constantly growing) stream.

After about five hours of hiking, Brother Green finally shouted through the wind and rain. "Here's the spot. Let's set up camp over in that clearing." The simultaneous dropping of six backpacks made a loud thud on the soggy earth.

We had reached exhaustion—and probably couldn't go another step. And just as we allowed ourselves time to relax, the rain stopped. Instantly. I glanced upward and couldn't help but think that we were just taught some important lesson that we wouldn't understand for years but we would be telling our kids during family night someday.

Setting up in the rain would have been extra miserable, and I was glad that we weren't fighting the elements anymore. But just because we weren't fighting the elements didn't mean we weren't fighting.

I was sharing a tent with Curt, mostly because everyone else already has a system in place for these kinds of campouts. JD and Mason shared a tent because JD was the only one who wasn't bothered by Mason's loud snoring. Doug and Ryan worked out a deal where Ryan would carry the tent, and Doug would provide an almost unlimited supply of Twinkies for Ryan.

That left the two new guys (me and Curt) to fend for ourselves. I wanted to sleep in a tent by myself, but Curt brought up the idea of sharing in the hallway at church while Mom was standing there. I got the "you better say yes" look and couldn't back out. So I was stuck setting up the tent with Curt while he spouted off about how it had rained *every day* on his brother's mission to Costa Rica. I stopped listening when he said "Costa Rica" with a forced Spanish accent.

Once the tent was standing, I realized that listening to my mom was a mistake. It would have been worth getting grounded for a week or two just to avoid this mess. For one thing, Curt's sleeping bag was one of those shiny kinds that makes a loud noise whenever it rubs against the sleeping pad. He also unloaded about seven or eight small bags of chips, mostly the really smelly kind like Funyuns, Ranch CornNuts, and Hot Cheetos. I don't know how he had room for the chips in his backpack . . . but I knew that there wouldn't be room enough in this tent for me to stay sane.

This was a good opportunity to rest, so I lay down on my sleeping bag to stretch out my legs. Jacob's pillow was perfectly soft and cold. I could easily fall asleep and not wake up until tomorrow. But once I stopped moving, I got hungry. Fast. Dinner wouldn't be for another few hours, and my stomach growled in annoyance. All I had eaten on the trail was a flattened PB and J sandwich and a granola bar. Curt crunched away on his CornNuts so loudly that I couldn't even think anymore. I needed to get my mind off food.

"I'm going out to see what everyone else is up to." I'm not even sure if Curt heard me over his crunching.

The air outside felt so different from the hot, stale air back home. There was a dusting of fog near the trees, and the birds were starting to chirp after the morning downpour. I decided to sit on a soggy tree stump and carve a little stick into something—nothing fancy, probably just a smoother stick. I'm not really a great artist, and I've gotten used to not having my art projects displayed on the bulletin boards in the hallway at school—I'm okay with it.

Curt came out of the tent, dusting the CornNut residue off his hands. "You have your Totin' Chip?" It was more of an accusation than a question.

"My *what*?" I had no clue what he was talking about. "I don't have any chips, but I'm sure you have plenty to—"

He cut off my attempt at sarcasm before it came out. "It's the card that says you're allowed to use a knife in Scouts." He reached into his pocket and pulled out a business card–sized certificate with his name on it. He shook it like one of those old Polaroid pictures. "You need to get one of *these* . . ." He inserted a dramatic pause. "Before you can use *that*," he finished, pointing at my knife.

"Well, I guess I'll just have to take my chances." What a killjoy. I'd never even heard of the Totem Pole Card, or whatever it is. How was I supposed to have one? I was seriously considering sleeping on my own without a tent and taking my chances with Mom when I got home.

Just then, a bright-pink flash came jutting out from the tree line. JD slid to a stop in front of us, and he looked irritated. "It's about time you guys finished. We're ready to play capture the flag. Let's go." And just like that, Curt and I were recruited to play the most classic camp game of all time. I just hoped I didn't have to be on JD's team— I'm pretty sure he could be seen from outer space with that poncho on.

Decoy

Jensen, you're with us. Curt and JD, you're with Doug. You've got five minutes to hide your flag and get set up. Here's your flag." Mason tossed an old Webelos neckerchief to JD and turned to march into the soggy forest. I guess capture the flag is the one thing that can pull Mason out of his everyday coma—he sure was wide awake now. He was moving fast, though, so I hurried to catch up before he disappeared into the trees.

And he could have disappeared easily. He was decked out in a full camouflage suit, the kind that Army Rangers wear to make it look like they're covered in leaves. His face was smeared with black and green paint, making only his eyes visible. (And I'm assuming his teeth too, but I couldn't tell because he wasn't in the mood to smile.). I was trying to figure out how he fit that entire getup into his backpack . . . and I came to the conclusion that he must have left his sleeping bag at home. Mason doesn't need much help sleeping, anyway.

"Jensen, which flank you want?"

"Umm, how about the . . . uh . . ." I really had no clue what he was talking about, but I wasn't about to ask a stupid question to a nearly invisible guy that could very well have a sniper rifle on him. Not to mention the fact that he sounded like Mr. Flacco, our PE teacher, when he called me "Jensen."

"Which *side* do you want?" His exposed eyes rolled in annoyance.

"Oh, yeah. I'll take the right side, er . . . flank," I said, pretending to know exactly what that meant.

Ryan chimed in with "I'll take the left," but I'm pretty sure that he didn't know what "flank" meant either.

Mason finished tying our flag (a maroon paisley bandanna) to a broken limb and turned to face us. "I'll go down the middle—they'll never see me. You guys stay on the flanks and *don't* lose sight of our flag—no matter what." Ryan and I nodded in unison, and the adrenaline began to pump through my body. I stuck my hand out, thinking that we'd do some sort of cheer like we used to do before soccer games, but Mason was already gone.

I took my post on the right flank about twenty yards from our flag, where I knelt down on the wet leaves behind a giant tree with a split trunk. I had to rest my chin in the crevice between the two trunks just to see anything. I felt like an acorn ready to be fired from a giant slingshot.

Nothing happened for a good ten minutes. I was watching a glossy beetle scurry in and out of the bark when something in the forest caught my eye. It was that unmistakable pink poncho, and it was about fifty yards directly ahead of me. I tried to get Ryan's attention, but he was lying down on his stomach, facing the other direction. I had to make a decision.

Ryan was in position to tag anyone who came close to our flag, so I wasn't really needed here. I could sneak over to where JD was hiding, tag him, and free up myself to look for *their* flag. Mason would be happy to have one less person hunting him, especially since JD was probably the only one who could catch him in a chase. I decided it was worth leaving my post to take JD out of the game.

I chose to go even farther out to the right side before going in for JD. I figured he would be watching the middle of the battlefield, allowing me to sneak up behind him. I tried one more time to get Ryan's attention by throwing a couple of small rocks, but he wasn't looking my way. I decided to go for it.

I sort of tiptoe ran to another tree that was just a few yards away. The rain-soaked earth absorbed most of the noise from my feet—sneaking up on someone wouldn't be a problem today. I kept repeating the process of running to a new tree, pausing for twenty seconds, and running again. I was making great progress, and JD hadn't moved since I started. Everyone always talked about Mason and JD being almost impossible to find in capture the flag— but here I was, about to win the game for my team as a brand-new deacon. That's the kind of news that will definitely make it back to Sunday School.

That adrenaline hadn't worn off yet, and I tried to stop myself from shaking as I inched closer to the sitting duck. There he was, crouched down in a small grove of ferns. The tail of his bright poncho was fluttering in the breeze—I don't know *how* he thought we wouldn't see him. When I got within twenty feet, I made the charge. From this distance there was no way he could get up in time to outrun me.

I ran at full speed, dodging a few boulders and low branches along the way. I reached him so quickly that he didn't even have time to move! I reached down to touch his shoulder, and I couldn't hold back a big smile. "Gotcha!"

But my hand met no resistance, and I toppled awkwardly into the ferns. A thick smell that reminded me of a new shower curtain surrounded me, and I realized that I was lying facedown on a hot pink floor. JD's poncho.

But there was no JD. Before I could even register that I had fallen for a decoy, I heard the cheering. "We got it!" JD was running back with our flag, Curt nipping at his heels. Doug jumped out from behind a thick boulder to give them high fives, and they couldn't stop laughing.

Mason popped up from the middle of a clearing just ten feet to my left and scared me half to death. He didn't say a word; he just glared at me with those uncamouflaged eyes.

"I thought *this* was JD," I said as I showed him the wadded up poncho in my hands. It even sounded pathetic to me, so I continued, "I thought Ryan could protect the flag by himself."

"I told you not to leave the flag." Yep, his teeth *were* visible, because now he was grimacing, and from the agonized look on his face, you'd have thought he just lost the Little League World Series or found out it was fish stick day at lunch or something. "Where *is* Ryan, anyway?" He turned his disappointment in the other direction, and that was fine with me.

"I don't know. He *was* over by the flag. *Ryan!*" He didn't answer, so we walked back to our starting area. "There he is," I pointed to where Ryan was hiding on the ground. He wasn't on his stomach anymore—he was sort of curled up on his side with his forearms covering his face. "Hey, Ry—"

Mason threw his hand up to cut me off.

"SHHH! *Look* . . ." He pointed at a light brown rock about the size of a football near Ryan's knees. Only it wasn't a rock. It was a bristling porcupine.

PG Words

I'm not sure who was more frightened—Ryan, the porcupine, or me. The thing was barely bigger than Becky's Yorkie (the one who always poops in our front yard), but then again, Becky's Yorkie doesn't have a thousand needles sticking out of its rear end. When it noticed us, it began thrashing its pincushion of a tail back and forth furiously. It had turned to face Mason and me and was now standing parallel to Ryan, their faces almost even. As it backed up, though, it was moving right toward Ryan's bent legs. I'd seen *Old Yeller* enough times to know what happens to dogs who mess with porcupines, and this didn't look good for Ryan. They had to shoot Old Yeller . . .

Ryan tried to roll away from the moonwalking porcupine but was trapped by a stand of five or six aspen saplings behind him. Mason stomped toward the porcupine, yelling at the top of his lungs. I followed his lead. "Hey! Get out of there! *Git!*" I clapped my hands to add to the noise level. Mason was trying to whistle in between shouts, but he was only able to produce loud wind noises. Ryan yelled too, but his shouts were drenched in desperation.

"Wait! *Wait!*" Ryan tried one last time to reason with the porcupine, but it was too late. The porcupine backed straight into Ryan's thigh, and it turned its head as if to watch Ryan's reaction. Ryan let out a scream that pierced the entire forest before gradually fading to an almost inaudible whisper. He gasped for breath and then screamed again. This time he mixed in some choice PG words for the porcupine, who was already scurrying away from the scene—no doubt with a smirk on its face. Ryan was turning in circles on the ground, clenching his right leg with both hands.

"Dude, stop spinning around." Mason was on the ground trying to see the damage. Dozens of quills stuck out of Ryan's right thigh, and a pool of dark blood was beginning to form a circle on his tan shorts. "Settle down. We have to take out the needles." I'm not sure if Mason knew what he was doing or not, but I didn't have a better solution at the moment. By now, the other boys had arrived behind us.

"Whoa . . . *what* did that? A porcupine?" JD and the others leaned in for a closer look.

"No, it was a skunk, genius." Ryan had never been one for sarcasm, but his injury was giving him a bit of a mean streak. I had to give him props for that one.

JD didn't catch the insult, though. He turned to Doug and whispered, "Are we gonna have to suck the poison out?" Doug just shook his head.

Mason reached underneath his camo suit and pulled out a Leatherman tool. I looked back to see if Curt was going to ask him for some ID, but he was just watching the scene, eyes wide.

Mason tried to unfold the pliers with one hand like the guys with the butterfly knives in those old gangster movies. It didn't unfold, though, and he waved his arm around for a good thirty seconds, trying to get it opened. He glanced up to see if we were watching before he awkwardly used his other hand to open up the Leatherman.

That little display prompted Doug to kneel down next to Mason. "You know what you're doing?"

"Yep. Just need to pull out the needles. We should get 'em out in time for one more game." This was Mason's last-ditch effort to save his teammate so he could even up the score in capture the flag.

He pinched the first quill with the pliers and pulled it with a quick jerk upward. Ryan screamed. More PG words. He hit Mason on the shoulder three quick times before Doug intervened.

"Maybe we should bring him back to camp."

Mason looked at the wound on Ryan's leg, glared at the bandanna in JD's hand, and settled his gaze back on Ryan. He finally gave up. "All right. But who's gonna carry him?"

"We all will. It's only a little ways back to camp." Doug helped Ryan to his feet. Ryan tried to take a step on his wounded right leg and almost collapsed back to the forest floor. Doug was able to stabilize him and turned to me. "Andrew—help." I hurried to Ryan's side. He draped

37

his arms around our shoulders, but he had to take all the weight off his good leg just to get down to our height. I grunted under the added weight and felt like someone had loaded one of those big sacks of concrete directly onto my right shoulder. After I adjusted my stance a bit, Doug and I were able to start walking in unison toward the camp. A few moments later, we were making good progress, and Ryan seemed to be cheering up a bit.

"We're almost there," Doug said. But then we caught a glimpse of the same dang porcupine jutting out of a bush ten yards in front of us. Ryan's eyes widened, and he dragged his feet on the ground to stop our progress. The sudden momentum shift caused Doug to bump his own leg into Ryan's collection of porcupine quills, and things went south in a hurry.

Ryan groaned in pain and twisted his body to alleviate the sting. He let go of Doug and put me in a hold-on-for-your-life type of headlock. A tree root held on to my foot, and we hurtled to the ground. Ryan and I landed simultaneously, only I was sandwiched between him and a rocky patch of earth.

My face was wedged against a flat rock the size of a Frisbee, and I could feel a searing hot pain above my left eye. I pried my arm out from underneath Ryan and tried to rub away the pain. I examined my fingers to see if there was blood, but there was only a tiny bit. Even so, the raw, painful patch of former skin convinced me that I had a big raspberry on my forehead.

Ryan was rolling on the ground again, too hoarse to scream anymore. Curt and JD had already made it to camp and came running back with Brother Green and Brother Campbell. They had a small first aid kit and knelt down next to Ryan to assess the damage.

"It doesn't look that bad, Ryan. We'll get you fixed up." Brother Green's calmness seemed to help Ryan. I couldn't blame him for freaking out earlier . . . when your life is in the hands of a couple of deacons, things probably look pretty bad. Brother Campbell gently helped Ryan up into a sitting position and gave him some Advil and water.

Brother Campbell turned and noticed the scrape on my head. "You okay, Andrew?"

"Yeah. It just stings a little." I touched it again to see if it was gushing blood. It wasn't.

"Let's clean it up. You have all kinds of dirt in there." He pulled out an alcohol wipe from the first aid kit and handed it to me. "You can clean it out with this." I took the wipe and gently stroked it on the scrape. I wasn't expecting the sting to be so sharp, but I tried not to let on that I was in serious pain. Brother Campbell just watched the whole time. I wished he would turn away so I could at least whimper in private.

Brother Green was busy cutting off the tops of all the quills in Ryan's leg, leaving just about a half inch sticking up above his shorts. "We'll pull these out in a minute, but we're going to have to cut your shorts to get the rest of the quills, okay?"

Ryan looked worried. "I didn't bring any other pants."

"I'm sure someone has some extra." He turned to the gallery of spectators. "Anyone have some extra shorts for Ryan?"

"I do." Curt started running back toward the camp. Brother Green looked at Ryan, who nodded once to give approval. He grabbed a pair of tiny silver scissors from the kit and cut through the right leg of Ryan's shorts—revealing a bit of bright blue underpants. Turns out I'm not the only one with leftover Transformers underwear.

Curt reappeared with a pair of red basketball shorts for Ryan. I recognized them as part of the uniform we had on our fourth grade Parks and Rec team—they were no doubt too small for Curt, let alone Ryan. Ryan examined the shorts and lay back down with his eyes closed . . . probably trying to forget this day ever happened. Brother Green let out a soft chuckle as he pulled the last quill out.

Weak and Simple

Ryan was struggling just to get the words to the hymn right at our first of three nightly devotionals. The right side of his face was painted with five or six long scrapes that went from chin to ear, and his right thigh was bandaged with half a roll of gauze. That, combined with his already butchered hands from the Beehives-at-the-parking-lot incident, made it nearly impossible for him to sit comfortably. The poor guy kinda just lay on his back and propped himself up by his elbows. The only thing between his backside and the ground was a pair of child's shorts.

After the hymn, Doug gave the shortest prayer I'd ever heard—it was six seconds, max. Brother Campbell was still bowing his head when Mason hopped up to gather more firewood. Eventually, Brother Campbell looked up. I imagine he had been adding his own prayer to Doug's.

He took a deep breath and started to give an introduction to his lesson. He felt around blindly under the chair for his scriptures, and when he found them, papers fell out and scattered all over the ground. Finally, he gathered it all together and began.

"Tonight I want to talk to you guys about—" But that's as far as the talk went. Mason, still hidden beneath his "ghillie" suit (he corrected me after I called it a "camouflage outfit"), dropped a log the size of a kitchen garbage can on top of the fire.

Crack! The fire expanded with furious speed, and ashes and flaming bits of wood exploded into the air in all directions. Those who were sitting closest had to roll away to avoid a direct hit. Even with all of the confusion, the only sound I heard after the explosion came from JD.

"*Dude!*" JD cowered away from Curt, who was slapping violently at his back. "What are you doing? Get off me!" He pushed his way off the log they were sharing and stood back, panting with rage.

"You were *on fire*! I was trying to put it out," Curt defended. We all looked in unison, and JD strained his neck to see the backside of his shoulder. Sure enough, there was a softball-sized hole with black edges on the right shoulder of his poncho.

Curt continued in anger. "Why are you still wearing that *stupid* thing anyway? It's not even raining." Now he was on the verge of tears, and JD stared silently at his poncho.

Then Curt turned his anger to Mason. "What the heck were *you* thinking? Why would you throw that thing on the fire?"

"A fire needs wood, Einstein!" Mason yelled back at

Curt, bristling just like the porcupine did earlier. Everyone else made it worse by trying to break up the argument. Even Ryan got into the mix, although he didn't bother to get up. Any spiritual feelings that may have been brought in by the opening song were long gone.

Brother Campbell stepped between Mason and Curt. They weren't really in a fistfight. They were acting more like two dogs being held back by their owners' leashes (only nobody was really holding them back). Brother Campbell managed to silence the shouting, but then he looked around, not quite sure what to do. Brother Green seemed content to let him handle it. Another one of those scoutmaster teaching moments, I guess.

He took a deep breath and put his arm around Curt. He looked at each of us one by one. "Let's try this again. Mason, thanks for the firewood, but I think we're good for a while now. JD, are you okay? You're not on fire anymore, right? Andrew, can you help me gather my papers?"

He was calm. Like my mom on my second grade field trip to the zoo. She had to think fast when the orang-utans started making obscene gestures, but Mom never flinched. *"Come along, guys, we need to go see the elephants before their nap time. Justin, look at this map and see if you can help me find the restrooms. Anyone want a cotton candy?"* Brother Campbell had the same smooth way about him.

As we were picking up his papers, he kept talking, but I don't think it was his originally scheduled lesson. "When I was on my mission, I had a companion who always liked to toast his bread for breakfast. Only it wasn't sliced bread, and we didn't have a toaster. So he used a frying pan. A really small one."

I picked up the last crumpled paper and handed it to him. He patted me on the shoulder and said, "Thanks, Andrew."

He continued the toast story. "Anyway, Elder McAllister would slice these mini French bread loaves in half and put them in the pan. They would always hang over the edge a bit, just because the pan was so small. McAllister always had to go to the bathroom too. So he'd usually start toasting his bread and then head in to take care of business.

"Well, this time, his 'business' must have taken longer than usual. I came in from the bedroom and saw that the entire pan of bread was on fire. I went to get a cup of water to throw on it, all the while yelling at McAllister to get in and help.

"Of course the water wasn't working that day. That happened quite a bit in our apartment, but it was just something we lived with. I grabbed the first thing I could find to try and put out this now huge fire. I used one of my shirts to slap at the stove top, but that didn't do anything but ruin my only clean shirt."

As Brother Campbell recounted his story, everyone in the circle was sitting perfectly still. Watching. Listening. *Smiling.* That hadn't happened much today.

"McAllister was able to find some soda, which must have been shaken up in the chaos. It exploded all over the place when he opened it, but eventually he was able to drench the fire as much as he had already drenched me."

"So there I was, a nineteen-year-old kid, covered in sticky soda, looking at a black stove top and holding what was left of a white shirt. I had to laugh at myself. I was so *weak*. I didn't understand the language, and I didn't understand the bus schedule. Heck, I didn't really understand much of anything."

He paused and looked at the ground for a good full minute. Then he lifted his shoulders, raised his head, and nodded slightly. "But I was called of God. He called me to be a missionary. Not my stake president, not my dad, not my Young Men leaders. *Me*. And if the Lord thought I was strong enough to do the job, then who was I to tell Him He was wrong?"

He reached down and dusted off his scriptures. He quickly found the page he was looking for and read, "That the fulness of my gospel might be proclaimed by the weak and the simple unto the ends of the world, and before kings and rulers.

"That was me. Now, it's you guys. *You* were called to do a great work. *You* have a strength inside of you that Heavenly Father knows. Don't ever forget that. The world may say you are weak, that you're simple. But Heavenly Father says you're strong. And He trusts you. So don't let Him down."

As he bore his testimony to close the meeting, all I could think about was how weak I really was. I couldn't even help carry Ryan back to camp without almost killing him. And that's just physical weakness. Spiritually I was even worse. I could *never* find a scripture like Brother Campbell did, even if I knew where it was. I don't know if it was the Spirit or just self-pity, but I choked back some thick, hot tears.

And during the closing hymn, I was the one who couldn't get the words right.

Mosquito's Bite

Morning came. Slowly.

Curt's sleeping bag made that fabric-squeaking noise every time he shifted, which happened about every five minutes. But I can't blame Curt for all my sleep troubles. The wind was blowing nonstop, causing a whole slew of other strange noises—all of which somehow sounded like an approaching bear. It's hard to sleep when you're imagining a hungry bear sniffing your head through the tent wall.

I must have fallen asleep eventually, because I woke up to Curt spraying his armpits with some can that looked like hairspray.

"What are you *doing*?" I asked in my hoarse morning voice. Maybe this was some bizarre dream.

"Deodorant. You don't use it?" He snapped the lid back on the can and tossed it in his backpack. He wasn't even waiting for my answer.

I rolled my barely opened eyes. "*Yes.* But mine doesn't come from a spray can."

"My brother said that this is the best kind. And he played varsity football all through high school." He stood up and started buttoning his Scout shirt.

He was the backup kicker! I didn't say it out loud but wanted to. *And that doesn't make him an expert on deodorant, either.*

I pulled my sleeping bag over my face until the haze in our tent settled, then got up to get ready for the day. Curt finished getting his pack ready and unzipped the tent. It was amazing how quickly the tent warmed up when the sun came out. The fresh, cool air actually felt good.

"Don't forget to leave your sunscreen out. We'll be hiking along the river pretty much all day. Probably won't be much shade." With that, Curt rezipped the tent from the outside.

Thanks, Mom. I was beginning to regret not actually saying these thoughts out loud. Regardless, I put some sunscreen on before I forgot. I guess I was supposed to pack up the tent by myself—must be some unwritten rule about being the last one out. I packed my bag, rolled up the tent, and headed over to the campfire area for breakfast.

Everyone but Mason was already done eating, and they were lined up playing a game of hand slap. Even Ryan was up and about, although he was walking with a limp. Worse than the injury was the fact that his shirt was a few inches longer than the bottom of his borrowed shorts. He looked like Paige or Kari on a Saturday morning, still wearing their nightshirts.

Mason was by the fire, getting his breakfast ready. I

pulled out my mess kit from the top of my backpack and found the ziplock baggie labeled "Wednesday Breakfast." It wasn't much—a granola bar, a box of raisins, and a tortilla. I noticed Mason toasting his tortilla on a rock in the fire, but I decided to eat mine raw. I didn't care for the raisins, so I tossed them back into my backpack as I finished the granola bar.

"Ready, guys?" Brother Green was coming out of the trees and shaking out his toothbrush. "Let's hit the trail."

Before we started hiking, we had a prayer and a quick summary of what to expect that day. Brother Green let us know that we'd be hiking along the river for about six and a half miles, and that we'd stop at lunchtime to do a little fishing and maybe some swimming. He finished with one last reminder.

"Be sure to keep your sunscreen handy. There won't be much shade today." I didn't look at Curt, but I could tell that he was staring right at me. Nothing against Brother Green, but I would have given anything for an overcast day. Just to stick it to Curt.

And with that, we were on the trail. It was nice to be hiking without the rain beating us down, but we had something almost worse to deal with: mosquitoes. My ankles and shins were already plastered with itchy welts after just a few miles. Why didn't Curt tell me to leave out the bug spray? *That* would have been useful information.

At least I wasn't the only one suffering. Everyone was scratching or slapping their legs with almost every step. As we broke through another opening in the tree line, we saw the river for the first time. It weaved in and out of grassy banks, carving a path that spanned almost fifteen feet in some places.

Wow. Dad would love this place. One time we went on a family trip to the Grand Canyon, and I remember Mom and Dad arguing about whether we should go on a river raft trip or not. Mom won, I guess, because we ended up playing miniature golf at some campground instead. But I always remember how Dad said he would go river rafting someday . . . with or without us.

We hiked a little ways along the river until we found the "old log bridge," as Brother Green called it. It had been there when he was a kid, so I guess it was reliable enough, but it looked like sure death. The log was only about two feet above the water level, and it crossed the river at a fairly narrow part. It was maybe ten feet from end to end, but it seemed more like twenty to me.

"Easy," said Mason, and he scurried atop the three-foot-diameter log. He did a sort of crisscross stepping pattern all the way across—the kind we used to do in PE. It seemed a little dramatic to me.

When he hopped off the log on the other side, he glanced back to make sure we were watching. "You guys might need to crawl on your bellies—it's pretty hard to balance." He reached out to steady the 6,000-pound log, as if he was holding a ladder for his dad. I kinda thought he was right about the crawling, but for JD, Ryan, and Doug, he might as well have told us that riding a two wheeler bicycle is too hard and that we should keep the training wheels on.

"Pssh. Whatever. If you can do it, I can do it. Look

out." Doug walked quickly across the log with his arms straight out, like an airplane. Ryan and JD followed, neither skipping a beat. I looked back at who was left: just the two leaders and Curt. And I was next in line.

I hopped up on the log and started to walk slowly toward the other side. The water rushing below the "bridge" sure was loud, and I was finding it hard to keep my concentration. My mosquito bites began to itch like never before. Everything around me turned into a huge distraction, and I panicked. I was only four feet onto the bridge, but I froze up solid. The only thing I could do was lean forward and hug the log for dear life.

I heard Brother Campbell ask if I was all right, but I ignored him. I just held on tightly and slid myself forward a little at a time. I was almost to the end of the bridge when Curt stepped over my torso and hopped to the ground at the end of the log. He must have been able to walk across too. That left me as the only one who needed training wheels. And the mosquito bites just got worse.

When we finally stopped at the fishing hole, I didn't even think about lunch. I just wanted relief from the itchiness. We all must have had the same idea, because it was a full-on race to get in the water.

The mosquitoes couldn't handle the frigid water of the swimming hole. We shouldn't have been able to, either, but we all danced around in the three-foot pool, hugging ourselves for warmth. My lower body was so numb that not even the itching could be felt. I knew it wouldn't last, though, and that come bedtime I'd have one more reason to be awake all night.

The Accident

We hiked a few more miles after lunch and set up camp next to the river. I could tell that I'd have to use the bathroom all night, since all we could hear was the sound of rushing water. But this was pretty much the only flat area we'd seen all day. The river had led us into a narrow canyon with walls covered in pine and aspen trees. Our campsite was big enough for our tents and a small fire pit, but that was it.

According to the duty roster, my job was to collect wood for the fire. Ryan was assigned to help, so we set out into the dense trees to find some.

"So what's the deal with you and Becky?" He was looking right at me with a crooked smile.

"Nothing!" I think I might have responded a little too quickly. "What do you mean?"

"I mean, every time I ride by your house, you guys are out shooting hoops or riding scooters. That's what I mean." His smile was getting bigger.

"We've been friends for a long time." I shrugged my shoulders. "She's cool."

"Uh-huh. *Friends.*" He picked up a fallen branch to use as a walking stick, his smile gradually turning to a frown. "I guess after my flop yesterday, I don't stand much of a chance with Katie. I'm such an idiot."

"She probably already forgot," I lied.

"Yeah," Ryan said, only agreeing out of courtesy. He pulled out the folded-up index card from his pocket. He unfolded it, looked at it for a split second, and put it back. I didn't dare pull out the note Becky had written me, even though I had been carrying it since we'd started.

"Dude, when we're sixteen, we'll totally have to go on double dates and stuff," Ryan finally said.

"That would be . . . um . . . awesome," I tried to say with enthusiasm, but I don't think it worked.

Sheesh! I'd barely been a deacon for a week, and I was already getting roped into date nights? Even though sixteen seemed so far away and dating a girl was definitely the last thing I wanted to do right now, it *was* nice to have future plans with a real friend.

Before it got worse, I added, "And you'll have to come shoot hoops sometime." This was a subject I was more comfortable with. "But don't wear those shorts. Katie only lives three houses down from me."

Ryan looked down at his shorts and then threw his stick at me. We both laughed and used the stick as the beginnings of our woodpile.

We made it back to the camp just as the clouds started gathering. The sky went from bright blue to pale gray in a matter of minutes. The wind started blowing again too. Just what I needed to make dinner and sleeping so much more pleasant.

Our dinner was brief, and the evening devotional wasn't going to happen outside tonight. Brother Green said we should go to our tents and read our scripture handouts. He had given us each a few photocopies of various Book of Mormon scriptures so that we could leave our nice (and heavy) scriptures at home. We scattered to our tents before the big drops started falling.

I was zipping up the tent when I heard Ryan yelling, "Andrew!" I unzipped the tent to see Ryan running right at me. He stopped five feet short of the door and tossed me a Twinkie.

"I saved you a Twinkie. Doug brought a whole box of 'em." Then he turned and sprinted back to his tent.

"Thanks!" I yelled back, but I don't think he could hear me over the howling wind. I zipped up the door and turned to get settled in. Curt was already sitting in his sleeping bag, looking right at me.

I looked at the Twinkie, then back at Curt. "You want some of this?" I didn't want to share, but it only seemed right.

"No, I usually don't eat sugar right before going to bed." He turned his nose and shoved a handful of Cheetos in his mouth. I couldn't do anything but ignore him, and I was getting better at that with every hour.

I decided to get into my pajamas before having the Twinkie. I put on my gym shorts and found my scripture packet in my backpack before settling into my sleeping bag. The rain pelted our tent, and the wind constantly rattled the poles holding it up. Curt's lantern was bright enough for the whole tent, but I grabbed my headlamp just in case he finished early.

I turned to 2 Nephi 31 and opened the Twinkie. I took a big bite—probably a little too big because I had trouble breathing while I chewed it. I was about to take another bite when I heard the loud crack.

At first I thought it was some fireworks, or maybe something Mason and JD had done to the fire. But the loud crack was followed by a series of pops, then a deafening thud. The ground shook under me.

I looked at Curt, whose eyes were as big as tennis balls. We both scrambled to get out of our sleeping bags, and I unzipped the tent door. I didn't even put shoes on to step into the now sideways rain. Doug and Ryan were pointing and running toward the tree line, shouting something that I couldn't make out. Curt and I followed, my headlamp dimly lighting our path.

Doug had frozen in the middle of the path, both of his hands gripping the top of his head. Ryan had slipped in the mud, and small patches of wet dirt dotted his pale face. He was looking in the same direction as Doug, and I followed his gaze to the end of our little meadow.

The loud cracking noise had been a monstrous branch breaking off an old aspen tree. And that ground shaking thud must have come when the limb landed on Brother Campbell's small tent. I felt as if the wind had been knocked out of me as I took in the scene. Brother Campbell's lantern was still glowing behind the collapsed walls, and the unforgiving branch divided the tent in two. The light inside flickered twice and then went black.

Panic

Brother Green came from behind us, stopping himself by placing his hand on my shoulder.

"What was that?" he said, out of breath.

I didn't know how to answer. I just swallowed and looked back at the destroyed tent. He turned his head and looked in the same direction, and his grip tightened sharply around my shoulder. He released his grip after only a few seconds and sprinted to the collapsed tent.

"Jeremy! Can you hear me?" He was kneeling down, trying to determine where Brother Campbell was inside the tent. He found the zippered door on the ground and ripped it open. By now, our entire quorum stood in a semicircle around the scene—panic and rain dripping from our faces. I did the only thing I could think to do, which was shine my light where Brother Green was working.

He found Brother Campbell's head under the loose tent fabric and felt his neck for a pulse. Brother Campbell's eyes were closed, and he lay perfectly still, and I couldn't tell if Brother Green found a pulse or not. The giant log rested squarely on Brother Campbell's chest, which wasn't moving up or down. As my mind registered the scene, my stomach lurched, and I threw up my Twinkie. And other stuff.

I have never felt so absolutely worthless. A man was dying (or maybe already dead) right in front of me, and all I could do was hunch over and try not to spew on somebody. Brother Green was tugging at the log, but it wasn't budging. He surveyed the angles, took a deep breath, and searched for a plan. He paused and closed his eyes for no longer than a split second.

"Guys, I need your help," Brother Green said. He said it quickly and calmly, interrupting my own panicked thoughts. JD patted me on the shoulder, and all six of us moved in unison to our leader's side. Brother Green held up two fingers and pointed at each end of the fallen log. "Two guys on the end, two in the middle, and two on that end." Rain was pouring down, muffling the instructions. I squinted and listened as closely as I could—this was definitely not math class, and I really needed to pay attention here.

"Lift together on the count of three, and move the log *that* way." He pointed behind me. All of us turned our heads and stared into the dark forest as if the relief to this nightmare were somehow disguised in the trees. "Ready?" We snapped our attention back to the log and Brother Campbell underneath.

I wiped the remnants of the churned-up Twinkie

from my mouth and bent down across the log from Curt. We locked hands underneath the giant branch. I looked at Curt and nodded once—he did the same. Deep breath. The smallest branches on this thing were quite a bit bigger than my arms, and that wasn't a good sign. Brother Green counted, "One . . . two . . . three!"

I pulled upward with everything I had. The log still didn't move. I thought my forearm was about to snap in half, but I didn't stop. Curt's hands felt like slippery fish, and our grips were fading fast. I looked down at the two other pairs of deacons and Brother Green—they all looked like they were about to burst veins in their necks. I shut out the pain and promised myself (and Brother Campbell) that I wouldn't give up.

The chorus of grunting was all I heard, even though the rain roared all around us. Then, without notice, the log jolted up, probably about four inches from where it started. There was nothing gradual about it—it happened all at once. For the first time, I felt that we were making a difference. I forced my hands into a better grip on Curt's wrist, and the pressure on my forearm seemed to lessen. The log continued to move upward.

"This way!" Brother Green pulled the branch horizontally. We followed his lead, taking baby steps to the side. We made a slight pivot to coax the log off Brother Campbell and into a clear spot of ground. "Set it down slowly so it doesn't bounce back. JD and Ryan—you first, then Doug and Mason, then Curt and Andrew."

Now was not the time to be picked last. I silently urged the other guys to hurry—I couldn't hold Curt's fish-wrists much longer. We bent our knees to prepare for impact. Two by two the others set the log on the ground. That left me and Curt with the entire weight of the log in our slippery and tired hands. "Ready?" I shouted. "One . . . two—"

But Curt let go at about two and a half, and the weight of the log pulled me down to the ground. My knuckles were pinned between the log and the ground, and my rear-end pointed toward the sky.

"Sorry!" Curt raced behind me, put his arms around my waist, and tried to pull me free.

"Owww!" It felt like my elbows were going to snap. He must have heard me over the rain because he immediately let go. I was able to sink my hands farther into the wet earth and wiggle them out from under the giant log. We turned our focus to Brother Green, who was already working on Brother Campbell.

"He's breathing, but he's not doing good." He gently felt Brother Campbell's chest, arms, legs, and feet. "I think he's got some broken ribs and a broken leg. His head was banged pretty bad too. And he's in shock." That didn't sound good at all. He pretty much named every bad thing that can happen to your body. A pool of blood on Brother Campbell's leg was being washed away by the rain. Brother Green put both hands on the bloody spot and turned to face us for the first time.

"Andrew, let's use your tent. Go clear a space for him. The rest of you are going to help me carry him—just like we did with the log."

I turned to run, my heart pumping faster than my

legs. I concentrated on each step so that I wouldn't slip on the ferns that lined the pathway to my tent. The tent door was still unzipped, so I barely slowed down as I threw open the door and went to work. I unzipped both of our sleeping bags and put our pads together. I laid Curt's bag on the pads and put mine on top. In the end, it made a space about as big as my bunk bed at home.

I threw everything I could into my backpack and did the same with Curt's stuff. *Man, how many bags of chips did he bring?* There was a whole other stash behind his pillow. I tossed the bags near the doorway and stood back to make sure everything was acceptable. I think this would work as a hospital room or whatever it was going to be called.

"You ready for us?" It didn't matter if I was or not, because Brother Green and the rest of the boys were carrying Brother Campbell—and they weren't stopping. I held the door open as they gently set him on the dry bed. The floor was covered in muddy footprints, but for the most part, the bed and Brother Campbell remained clean.

Brother Green pulled out a vial of oil (just like my dad's) and prepared to give a blessing. Mason and Ryan were silently wiping up the muddy floor with their shirts. Doug had his hands pressed carefully on Brother Campbell's leg, so he was trying to wipe the rain off his forehead with his shoulder. JD held a flashlight up so everyone could see—but his hand was shaking uncontrollably. Curt was hunched over, dry heaving in the rain. I folded my arms, bowed my head, and began to cry.

Prayer

The rain didn't stop. After the blessing, Brother Green gathered us all together in Mason and JD's tent. I couldn't keep from looking toward my tent, wondering how Brother Campbell was doing. I guess all of us must have been doing the same thing.

"Hey, guys," Brother Green said, getting our attention. "He's going to be okay, but we have to make some decisions. He needs help—fast. So as soon as the rain lets up a bit, I'll hike back out to the car. That means you guys will have to take care of Brother Campbell. Are you okay with that?"

Curt opened the unzipped door to the tent and launched three more dry heaves. The rest of us stared blankly at Brother Green. Our silent response must have been interpreted as a "yes."

"Good. I'll stay with him until morning, just to make sure he's stable. I don't know if he'll wake up anytime soon, so you guys should get some sleep. I'll come wake you up before I head out." I found myself nodding non-stop but forced myself to be still after Brother Green hadn't spoken for ten seconds.

"Doug, how about you call on someone to say a prayer? I think we could use one right now." Oh man. I knew it was going to be me again.

"Andrew." Again, it wasn't even a question. Everyone was already bowing their heads before I could remind them that my last prayer about stopping the rain didn't work too well. I paused for a second to say a pre-prayer that I wouldn't cry during the main prayer. Confusing, I know. I was confused too.

I really don't remember exactly what I said to begin the prayer. I asked for Brother Campbell to be comfort-able and for us to be brave. Even though I wanted to ask for the rain to stop, I didn't dare try that again. As I continued, I thought back to what Bishop had asked in church—for the ward to pray for us. I pictured families kneeling and asking for Heavenly Father to watch over us. I remembered Kari saying our family night prayer and asking for angels to keep watch over me. Rather than let-ting my voice crack, I took a deep breath and decided to ask for the same thing.

"Heavenly Father, please send angels to help us. We need their help right now. We're scared. We don't know what to do. But we know that everything will be okay if we can get help." It wasn't exactly stake conference mate-rial, but it was the first time I remember having a real conversation with Heavenly Father. It was probably the first time I'd ever really needed anything other than help on a spelling test or help in finding a lost jacket.

When I said "amen," the fear was almost gone. But the rain kept falling.

In a "Crunch"

We all "slept" in Mason's tent. Mostly I just lay there, staring at the roof and listening to the patter of the rain. The sound of rain falling on the roof of my grandparents' cabin used to be one of my favorite things, but somehow I just didn't feel as safe as I did in that old cabin.

When the tapping came on the tent's door, all six of us sat up instantly—I guess none of us was sleeping. JD unzipped the tent to let Brother Green in. He was wearing a poncho and had his backpack strapped on.

"Hey guys, I don't think the rain is letting up very much," he said. Everyone paused and looked at me again.

Brother Green continued. "I'm going to head out now. Brother Campbell is doing fine, but he's still unconscious." He pulled out a scratched-up, yellow walkie-talkie and attached it on his hip.

"I've got you plugged into my GPS, so I'll be able to

find you guys again. But *don't* leave—you have to stay right here." He hit it against his palm and furrowed his brow as he pressed more buttons. If I'm being honest, I wasn't completely confident that that thing would lead him back to us.

"Someone should always be with Brother Campbell. When he wakes up, give him some of these Advil—it's not much, but it's all we got. He's going to be in some awful pain." He tossed a rattling plastic container to Ryan, who fumbled it several times before dropping it. "Keep him dry, and change the dressing on his leg wound every three or four hours. I left some strips of shirts in there with him." He looked up as if trying to remember any key details. "Any questions?"

I shook my head, although in reality I had about a hundred questions. *How long will you be? What if the Advil doesn't work? What if we have to amputate? Do we need a "Totem Ship"(or whatever it's called) to do that? What do we do if Curt doesn't stop barfing?* Curt was actually dashing toward the tent door at that very moment.

"All right then." Brother Green went around the tent and gave us each a hug. "You guys can do this. Remember the devotional? You aren't weak or simple. You're *strong.* And I know you'll have angels watching over you." He tapped the brim of my hat when he said that last part.

"Be strong, boys. I'll be back soon." He turned and jogged into the darkness.

Ryan and I took the first shift with Brother Campbell. The trail back to my tent was already filled with two inches of standing water, and it flowed steadily toward the river. In fact, the whole camp area was starting to look like an actual river. Since we were surrounded by steep canyon walls on every side, the runoff was bombarding our camp from pretty much the entire forest. The river was growing—and we were quickly becoming part of it.

Brother Campbell seemed fine. He whimpered every ten minutes or so, but other than that, he didn't show any signs of waking. We checked the bandage on his leg just to make sure it wasn't soaked in blood. Then we just sat there. I remembered the card that Becky had given to me, and I pulled it out of my pocket. It was soggy and faded, but I could make out the "Crunch" part of it. We really were in a crunch now.

After about thirty minutes, the water was so high on the tent walls that the poles began to rattle. It felt like we could easily be swept away any second, so I decided to break the silence.

"What should we do, Ryan?" I was looking for reassurance more than answers.

"I don't know. What do *you* think?"

"I think we need to move. Now." I was surprisingly confident in my response. This crunch we were in was teaching me to pray like never before. I had been praying almost nonstop ever since Brother Green left, and I felt like this was a clear answer. Maybe even a revelation. The same thought kept coming to my mind: *move*.

Ryan's eyes widened. "But that's pretty much the only thing Brother Green told us *not* to do. How will they find us?"

"I don't know, but I don't think we have a choice. We're about to be washed away. And he did say to keep him dry."

"How would we even carry him?"

My shoulders slumped—I hadn't thought that far ahead. I was too busy trying to convince myself that the thought to move was just my imagination. But it wasn't.

"I don't know." He had a point. There was *no* way we could carry him out of here. By the time Brother Green got back with help, we'd be up to our necks in water. And if the water did get worse, we wouldn't be able to keep Brother Campbell from drowning.

I had no idea what to do. We just sat there, waiting for more inspiration. I was straining my mind to listen for the answer—there had to be a way. Just then, we heard a voice outside the tent.

"Are you guys awake?" It was Mason. If we hadn't been awake, his loud barking would have made sure we were. For someone who sleeps through class five days a week, he sure did conjure up a lot of energy for campouts.

"Yeah," we answered in unison as Ryan unzipped the door. Mason and Doug were standing there, soaking wet.

"Check out what we made," Doug said, pointing to the ground. "It's a stretcher that the rescuers can use to get Brother Campbell out of here."

On the Move

I looked at Ryan, then back at Mason and Doug's contraption. It was a beautiful thing. They had lashed two long branches together at one end and then attached another, shorter branch between them at the other end, forming a big triangle. Mason's ghillie suit was stretched across the branches, making a taut platform for someone to lie on. It was just what we needed.

"We can't wait for the rescuers. We need to move Brother Campbell *now*," I blurted out. Again that same, strange confidence was in my voice.

Doug looked at me for a good ten seconds. "Let's do it. I think you're right." And just like that, we had a plan. Doug immediately started making assignments and putting the details in order. He, Mason, and Ryan would go pack up their things, and I would do the same here.

"We'll be back in five minutes." The three of them splashed back toward their tents.

Curt came running into our tent just a minute later.

"Doug said we're moving?" He had a panicked look on his face, and I didn't want to be the recipient of whatever was left in his stomach, so I tried to put a positive spin on things.

"Yep, but I don't think we're going far. They'll still find us in the morning, but we have to get out of this flood zone."

"Oh, okay." Spewage was temporarily averted. Curt looked down at Brother Campbell and then noticed his backpack sitting on the side of the tent.

"Thanks for getting my stuff together."

"No problem." It was my first non-sarcastic response to Curt—maybe ever.

We pulled the stretcher into the tent and put my sleeping bag on top of the platform. By the time we got everything ready for the transition, the other guys were there. They all had their backpacks on. The two tents were so wet that they couldn't really be packed, so they were quickly folded and lashed onto JD's and Ryan's backpacks.

Doug gave out the assignments. "Let's put him on the stretcher first, and then we'll take turns pulling him up the canyon—in groups of three." The others crouched down in the same spots they were in before, and I moved to the back to hold onto Brother Campbell's head.

"One . . . two . . . three!" We lifted him up and over to the stretcher, and it went much more smoothly than I thought it would. I grabbed my pillow (er—Jacob's pillow) and slid it between Brother Campbell's head and the branches.

JD wrapped a thin cord back and forth between the

legs of the stretcher to secure Brother Campbell in place. Mason tied two ends of a long rope around the front corner of the stretcher, making a loop about the size of a couple of hula hoops. He hopped inside the loop and put the rope over his chest—like he was about to bench press it. Doug stepped under the rope and stood next to Mason. "Andrew, put your backpack on and hop in." I felt like part of a mule team on one of those *Little House on the Prairie* episodes we used to watch for family home evening.

"Curt and Ryan, pack up the tent and catch up with us . . . we won't be going fast. JD, go ahead of us and find a trail. We're going *that* way," Doug said, nodding his head toward the canyon. "And turn your headlamps on."

JD put his pink poncho over Brother Campbell, covering his face and most of his body. And with that, we were off. The water was already up to my shins, and Brother Campbell's legs were completely submerged. But the stretcher actually slid pretty easily over the wet ground, and once we got some momentum, we made good progress. We switched mule teams when Curt and Ryan caught up. We switched every five minutes or so and didn't get too tired, even though we were going uphill.

Doug stopped us during one of the exchanges, about an hour after we left. "We need to go up there," he said, pointing up a steep cliff covered in ferns. It was probably twenty feet tall, and there was a thin ledge that gradually ascended to the top in a diagonal line. Even without the rain, the darkness, and the 180-pound leader on a home-made stretcher, that would be a difficult climb. But it was the only spot we'd seen so far that was even passable. Curt let one fly somewhere in the background.

Doug was on a mission to get Brother Campbell to the high ground, and he made sure we were too. "It's gonna take all of us to get him up there. There's only room on that trail for two to pull, and the rest of us are gonna have to keep the stretcher from falling over the ledge."

"JD and Ryan, you guys pull. Curt and I will push from behind. That leaves Andrew and Mason to stand next to the ledge and keep the stretcher on course." Oh, sure, why wouldn't I be the one on the ledge? I was waiting for him to call on me for another prayer when he continued.

"Leave your packs—we'll come get them once he's on top." With that, the Highland Fourth Ward Mountain Rescue Team was formed, and we stared up the wall of the most slippery, dangerous-looking cliff I'd ever seen.

High Ground

The pathway up the cliff was no more than three feet wide, and it was covered in sharp rocks. It was a straight shot up the side—no turns or switchbacks. But there wasn't really anywhere for me and Mason to stand, so we had to use the ledge of the trail as a hand hold and find an occasional outcropping of rocks to stand on.

With only a few feet left to go to the top, the stretcher started skidding off the muddy trail. Ryan and JD were holding the rope at the front, and the back of the stretcher started pivoting away from the canyon wall. If it continued on its current course, it would pull most of us down with it.

"I can't hold it!" Doug screamed. "Push it, Andrew!"

"I'm trying!" Only I had to try alone. Mason was about five feet in front of us, clutching a small bush to keep from falling.

"Get the back, Andrew!" Mason could see the whole

thing unfolding even though he was unable to move.

The corner of the stretcher slid over the edge of the trail and began to drop like a lever being pulled. I spotted the rock that I was just standing on a few minutes earlier, and I jumped to stand on it once again. The momentum from my jump caused me to lose my balance and teeter toward the depths of the canyon floor. There was no room on the path for my hands, and there was nothing to grab on to anyway. The only thing I could do was latch onto the lower branch of the stretcher. It gave way almost immediately. I felt Brother Campbell's leg slide over my wrist, and the momentum was about to take us both down the cliff.

How do you stop a lever? I had a split second to think of a plan. *Counterweights.* I don't know where the thought came from. In fact, I don't really know what counterweights are. But I knew exactly what to do.

"Guys, don't pull! Put your weight on the corners. Hurry!" I was fumbling to find a spot for my feet, but I couldn't quite reach the rock. I couldn't see if the others were moving to put their weight on the other side of the stretcher, so I yelled again. "Push down on the stretcher!"

The momentum pulling me downward stopped, and I found my footing on the small rock. I pulled my right arm from on top of the stretcher and slid it underneath, wedging it as far as I could. I put my shoulder under the corner of the stretcher and pushed up toward the ledge. "Now pull, guys!"

They were able to pull the stretcher parallel to the trail once again and stabilize its balance. Ryan and JD continued pulling until they were over the top of the canyon wall and beyond.

Curt reached down to grab my hand and pull me up to the vacant pathway. "Thanks, Curt," I said. He simply nodded. There was no more fear in his eyes . . . and not even a hint of puking.

"Nice save, dude," he said, out of breath. I had never heard him use the word "dude" before. He patted me on the shoulder and stood up on the trail. Doug was helping Mason onto the ledge, and we all walked down the trail to gather our packs.

"Hey, can you grab ours?" Ryan yelled from the top.

I waved and nodded, too tired to respond with words. I put my pack on one shoulder and Ryan's on the other. Doug grabbed his own and JD's, and Mason was already halfway back up the pathway with his.

From the top, the canyon looked like a raging river. We gave each other high fives and admired our ascent for a few moments. *How did we do that?* Something inside told me that we didn't do it alone. There's no way we should have been able to do that. *Angels.*

Doug turned to look at the high ground. "Let's set up over—" But Curt cut him off.

"Uh, guys—what's *that*?" He was pointing down, his pale face glowing in the rain. At the bottom of the canyon (right where we had left our backpacks) something moved.

It was a black bear, wading through the newly formed river.

Sausages

After a few minutes of discussion, our plan was simple. We would do exactly what we do best: be loud and obnoxious. I wasn't sure if the bear was male or female, but if it was a girl, we had a good chance of getting rid of it. Most girls don't want anything to do with a group of deacons.

While JD, Mason, and Doug set up the tents, Ryan, Curt, and I tried to make as much noise as possible.

Curt banged two aluminum pans he got from his mess kit. He was actually getting into a pretty good rhythm too. *BANG bang bang bang. BANG bang bang bang.* He started dancing around to the beat, looking up for two beats and then down for two beats. It reminded me of the American Indian exhibition at the state fair, only without the cool costumes. Or real dancing skills.

Ryan cupped his hands around his mouth and shouted things like "You don't wanna mess with us" and "We have . . . guns and stuff!" Even if the bear *could* understand human words, it would know immediately that Ryan was lying. Ryan couldn't keep his voice from wavering every time he said something like "We *eat* bears all the time at home."

I found a whistle in my first aid kit and blew it in four-second shifts. The three of us weaved in and out of a twenty-yard stretch at the top of the hill, constantly watching the canyon floor for signs of movement. Our symphony must have been annoying to the others, because they soon came to relieve us.

"We're going to set up an alarm, just in case the bear comes up here while we're sleeping," Doug said. Mason was already stringing a rope across the path's entrance to the top of the canyon wall.

"Tie these on the rope so that they're touching." JD handed out a bunch of forks, pans, a compass, and a few other things that would make noise when they touched. The line stretched between two trees about two and a half feet above the ground.

"That should do it," said Mason as he shook the rope with his hand. I could barely hear anything over the rain, but he seemed to think it would serve as an alarm if the bear came this way.

There were only two tents set up—and one was for Brother Campbell. "Where's the other tent?" I asked.

"It must have fallen off my pack on the way up the canyon. And I'm not going back down there to get it," JD said. "Does anyone want to volunteer to get it?"

There were a lot of heads shaking all at once. Curt

added emphasis. "Not with the be . . . the be . . . that *thing* down there." He still couldn't force himself to say the word.

Doug said, "Nobody's going down there with that bear." He glanced at Curt, who managed to stop a lurch midway.

"But where are we all gonna sleep?" Ryan was looking at the tent and counting something with his fingers.

"It'll be morning in a couple of hours," Doug said, looking at his wrist (which didn't have a watch on it, by the way). "We can all cram together for that long."

Blank stares. Raised eyebrows. Doug continued, "But someone has to stay with Brother Campbell." Before anyone could get a full word out, he finished, "I'll do it."

"I'll see you guys in the morning." And he was off with a skip in his step. The rest of us slowly marched to the other tent.

It was a little disturbing that Mason and JD had already neatly laid out all of our sleeping bags next to each other. They overlapped heavily on each side—this was going to be tight. And awkward.

Mason fell down on the far side of the tent, closing his eyes and drifting off to sleep almost immediately. There's the Mason I remember. One by one the rest of us slid into our sleeping bags. "Shouldn't we make sure Brother Campbell isn't bleeding? It seems like the bears will come swarming if they smell it," JD said.

"I don't think so. We're not worried about *sharks*. It's just a bear," I said as I slid between JD and Curt. I was pretty sure bears weren't like sharks, but not positive. JD seemed to accept the answer, because he didn't say anything else.

There wasn't even enough room for us to lie next to each other flat on our backs, so we coordinated our efforts to all lay on our left sides. In the end (after ten minutes of bumping heads and flinging impatient comments), we were settled.

Settled, that is, like a package of lean sausages. I couldn't move more than two inches in any direction—not even to scratch my head. The thought crossed my mind that a bear sure would love a nice tidy package of sausages, but I was too tired to be scared. Worse was the thought of this scene leaking out to the public. No doubt there would be news coverage of this whole thing—and the inevitable question, "What did you guys do last night?" I just hoped that everyone would keep their mouths shut and never utter a word of it to anyone. This is something that could ruin us if the priests and Laurels ever found out.

We just had to make sure that Ryan wasn't the one talking—he couldn't even lie to a bear.

A Five-Advil Situation

The light shining through the corner of the door let me know it was morning. It also clued me in to the fact that it wasn't raining anymore. I pushed Curt's arm off my face and sat up. It was eerily silent now that the rain had stopped.

Mason wasn't in his spot—how he was getting by with no sleep is beyond me. Everyone else was sound asleep. I stood up and accidentally stepped on JD's leg, but he didn't budge. There was so little room in the tent that when I lifted my foot off his leg, the only place to put it down to catch my balance was on Curt's stomach. Dangerous, considering the amount of puke he has churned up in the past twelve hours, but he just rolled over and groaned a bit.

When I finally reached the tent door, I could hear something moving just a few feet outside of the door. Something's footsteps were crunching leaves and small pebbles. The noise paused every few seconds, and I heard what sounded like sniffing.

"Mason?" I whispered loud enough for whatever it was to hear me. It went silent for a few seconds, and then the noises continued. Just crunching, pausing, sniffing. The bear. I knew it. It was wandering around camp, trying to find the package of sausages. Who knows what happened to Mason.

I scampered back toward the middle of the tent to wake up the others.

"Guys, the bear is back. Get up!" I shook Curt with one hand and JD with the other. JD snapped up violently from a deep sleep.

"What? Yes. The Skittles are in the glove box. But the grass stain won't come out." He was looking around frantically.

I wasn't about to respond to *that*. We just stared at each other for a while until he gradually recognized his surroundings. He looked a little embarrassed. "Oh, hey, Andrew. What did you say?"

"The bear. I think it's outside." He pulled himself out of the sleeping bag and stood beside me. The two of us hunched over to listen. "You hear that?" I pointed in the direction of the sniffing.

"We have to look," JD said as his shaking hand reached slowly for the zipper. He unzipped the door about six inches and backed away. I guess it was up to me to look. I pried the fabric apart and slid my face up to the screen.

"Dude, it's just Mason." I flung my hands up in disgust. Mason was crouched down like a catcher in baseball, touching the ground and looking into the woods.

JD put his hand on his head and lay back down on his sleeping bag, muttering something I couldn't understand.

I unzipped the door the rest of the way and stepped into the cool morning air. "Why didn't you answer me when I called your name?"

He still didn't answer, but he did start talking.

"Look at all these tracks. The bear came through here last night."

I looked at the patch of ground he was examining, which was full of clean lines in the shape of peanuts.

"Those are *our* tracks, Mason. From last night."

"I know, but if you were a bear trying to eat us, wouldn't you try to come in without leaving a bunch of evidence?" I rolled my eyes and walked away when he scooped a piece of mud from the ground with his fingers and lifted it to his nose to smell. At least I *hope* it was mud.

"You wanna help me hunt for breakfast? I bet there are a ton of squirrels and rabbits around here," he asked.

"I didn't think we were supposed to hunt things."

"Well, yeah, normally. But we're in *survival* mode now." He was wiping the "mud" off his hands. He picked up a walking stick that had been carved into a sharp spear and tossed it back and forth between his hands.

"Um . . . I think I still have all my granola bars and stuff. I'm good." Survival mode? We ate dinner less than twelve hours ago, and we still had a few days' worth of food left. That was a bit of a stretch, even for Mason.

He nodded solemnly and then crept stealthily into the forest under the cover of his camo. If we got out of this, I guessed that he was going to be the host of one of those

Discovery Channel shows where they just drop you in the forest with a cameraman and tell you to try to get out alive.

I made my way over to Brother Campbell's tent. Doug was lying on his poncho just outside of the tent, holding his Book of Mormon printouts.

"Did you sleep *out here* last night?" I'm sure the grimace on my face was noticeable. That would not be my idea of a good night—considering the rain, the bugs, the *bears*.

"Nah, I just came out here when the rain stopped. I mostly just sat up and read. I've never really read this, you know. But it's pretty dang cool."

"Yeah, it is. How's Brother Campbell?"

"He's all right, I think. Still breathing and stuff."

"I wonder when he'll wake up," I looked at the tent and tried not to think the worst.

The rest of the morning was pretty uneventful. Mason didn't catch anything with his spear (thank goodness). Ryan and JD tried for an hour but couldn't get a fire started. Curt was trying to make a "radio" out of his flashlight and the aluminum foil from some of Doug's Ding Dongs, but obviously he didn't get any signals. We all took shifts sitting with Brother Campbell, and it just sort of happened that whoever was "on call" would read Doug's Book of Mormon printouts.

During my shift, I was reading about Abinadi. I kept thinking back to the "weak and simple" scripture from the devotional. I don't think Abinadi was weak at all, but King Noah sure did. He wasn't one of the priests and didn't have any respect in the community. But he was the one called to deliver the message.

I was about to start another section when a scream came from inside the tent. It pierced the still afternoon air and made me jump.

"Ahhhhhhhhhhhhh!" Brother Campbell was awake, and something was wrong. I unzipped the tent and saw him on his side, clutching his broken leg. He heard me open the door and turned to face me.

"And . . . rew. Wha . . . happn'd?" He was breathing hard in between syllables, and the frightened look on his face must have matched my own.

"A tree branch fell on you last night. We had to move you because of the flooding." I was kneeling at his side now, searching for a way to help.

He shifted his weight to turn over. Bad idea.

"AHHHHHHHHHH!" His face contorted in severe pain, and he screamed again until he started coughing violently. I grabbed the half-filled water bottle from Doug's backpack and put it in his hand.

"Drink this." He couldn't hold on to it and the water spilled on the tent floor. I picked it up and pressed the bottle to his lips. He sprayed the first sip back into the air, but was able to take a small drink. I gave him the rest of it, and the coughing stopped.

The other guys were now at the door, watching the scene unfold.

"My head . . . is . . . feels like it's . . . exploding." He didn't look good.

"Here's the Advil." Ryan tossed me the container.

"We need more water," I said as I fumbled to open the container. Curt jumped in with a full bottle of water in his hand.

"Thanks." I put five Advil in my hand—I've seen my dad take three of these when his back is hurting, and this seemed like at least two Advil worse than that. "Here's some medicine, Brother Campbell." I put the pills in his mouth one at a time while Curt helped him sip some water.

In the movies they show the medicine work right away, but this wasn't the movies. He writhed in pain for another half hour before he finally fell back asleep.

He woke up like this three more times, each time in more agony. He wasn't going to last long. He needed something more than Advil—something we didn't have. It was going to be dark in about an hour, and I had the feeling that it would be a long night.

I handed the Book of Mormon pages to Ryan at the shift change. I decided to walk down to the edge of the canyon, just to see the path we climbed up last night. There was a weird echo in the canyon—and it sounded like another storm was coming. I couldn't really see the sky because of the thick tree cover, but I could definitely hear the thunder in the distance.

Great. More rain is *just* what we needed.

I had just turned to head back to camp when I noticed that the thunder wasn't really stopping. It just kept rolling—and getting louder. I walked back to the edge of the canyon and listened more closely. Ratatatatatat. It wasn't thunder at all.

It was a helicopter.

Nobody Notices a Deacon

I ran back to camp at a pace that would make even Mr. Flacco (my PE teacher) proud. "It's a helicopter. It's a helicopter," I said in my best Paul Revere voice.

Doug had a skeptical look on his face as he looked into the sky. "Are you sure? It could just be thunder."

"I'm sure. Over by the canyon you can totally tell it's a helicopter." The others had gathered around, eyes glued to the heavens. It started sinking in. We were going to be rescued without having to spend another night out here. That's when the smiles started to appear.

We gave each other high fives and awkward hugs. The hooting and hollering grew fast, but it came to a brief pause when Ryan started doing some sort of Riverdance, which none of us knew he could do. It was way too polished to be something he just made up.

"What? My mom made me take three years of clogging," Ryan defended. I filed that one away for future reference—just in case he couldn't keep his mouth shut about our sleeping arrangements last night.

Curt was still looking at the sky, then turned back to us. "How do we flag it down?"

"We gotta find a clearing. Come on." Mason was already leading the way. We ran until we reached a small meadow. It was no bigger than the infield of a baseball diamond, but it was the only place where we could even see the sky. The tall aspen trees were in full bloom, creating a ceiling with a small square opening above.

We raced out into the clearing and started jumping up and down, waving our arms furiously. The sound coming from the helicopter wasn't getting louder anymore. In fact, it seemed like it was fading into the opposite direction.

"It's leaving," I whispered to myself, hope fading just as fast as it came. "It's leaving!" This time my voice was much louder and much more desperate.

"What? It can't leave yet. They haven't found us." Ryan was still jumping up and down, but now he was scowling at me. "Keep waving—they'll see us."

"No, they won't." It was Curt, speaking boldly from behind us. I was waiting for him to tell us what his brother would do—no doubt he was a helicopter pilot in addition to his busy calling in the bishopric. But he just stated the facts. "They'll never see us down here. And it's going to be dark in thirty minutes."

I glanced back toward camp, thinking that we couldn't make it another night—Brother Campbell couldn't make it another night.

JD took off back toward camp, waving his arms to the sky the whole time.

"We've gotta get higher—above the tree line," Doug said, pointing to the tall aspens. "It's our only hope. And we probably only have a few minutes before the helicopter turns around."

Mason had an idea. "I can climb one of these trees."

We gathered around a tall aspen tree with hundreds of horizontal branches acting as a ladder to the sky. The only problem was that the first "rung" of the ladder was at least twelve feet up.

JD came running back into the clearing, holding his bright pink poncho. "You'll need this." He grabbed Mason's hiking stick/spear and weaved the sharp end in and out of the poncho, creating a flag. "It's like the Title of Liberty," he said, smiling. The photocopies of the Book of Mormon our leaders gave us were having a big impact on our survival—I made a note to remember that for a future family night lesson.

"But how are we gonna get Mason up to that tree?" I didn't want to be the stick in the mud, but it was a long way up. And we were running out of time.

"We could build a ladder," Curt suggested.

"We don't have time," said Doug.

Ryan clenched his fists and curled his lips in. "I'll be the ladder. Andrew, get on my shoulders." He crouched down with his hand on the tree trunk. "Get on!"

I mounted his shoulders, and he slowly stood up, like a newborn deer trying to get its balance. I almost toppled headfirst into the ground but barely managed to stop our forward progress by grabbing the tree trunk. When Ryan regained his balance, he gave more instructions.

"Doug and Curt—push him up our backs." What? This plan was sounding worse and worse. I guess the others thought the same, because they didn't do anything right away.

"Push him up!" Ryan wasn't messing around. He patted his rear end twice before he almost lost his balance again and had to grab the tree. Doug and Curt each made a platform for Mason's feet by interlocking their fingers. Mason stepped into the makeshift stirrups and grabbed onto my shoulders.

They hoisted him as high as they could, and Mason scrambled to get his knees on my shoulders. My head was pressed against the tree bark, and my shoulders burned with pain. One leg at a time, Mason stood up on my shoulders. Our balance wasn't real solid, like three dominos stacked vertically on a tennis ball.

Mason grabbed the lowest branch with both arms and relieved the pressure on my shoulders. "Got it!"

Ryan backed away and leaned forward, allowing me to hop off. He collapsed to the ground, grimacing with pain. "Nice, Ryan. That was awesome."

JD tossed the hot-pink Title of Liberty up to Mason, and he began his ascent up the tree. It was slow going at first because of all the smaller branches in the way. We cheered him on from the bottom, everyone telling him to go a different way.

The deep sounds of rolling thunder began to fill the air. The helicopter was returning. Our cheers turned to desperate pleas for Mason to hurry. He still had about twenty feet to go, and the helicopter was getting closer every second.

Mason seemed to float up the last section of tree. He hopped from limb to limb easily and much more quickly than before. Just as he was about to make the last push, he dropped the flag. But instead of falling, the wind gusted and pinned it against the trunk of the tree. Mason was able to reach down with his foot and snag the hood of the poncho.

By this point, each of us on the ground had our hands on our heads, fingers interlocked. There were a lot of deep breaths. The noise from the helicopter was louder than ever—it had to be close.

Mason crowned the tree just as we saw the bright-yellow aircraft over our meadow. He extended the flag and waved it back and forth, almost losing his balance several times.

The helicopter didn't stop—it just kept going in the direction of the canyon. But Mason didn't stop either. Just when the helicopter passed completely over the clearing, it stopped. The tail stayed completely still, and then backed up just a bit. It made a 180-degree turn and positioned itself directly above us.

There, in the passenger seat, was a man in a green jumpsuit. He was speaking into his headset and pointing his finger right at us. He turned to the pilot and then back at us. He had a big smile on his face and gave us a thumbs-up.

"Welcme" Home

I know what you're thinking. We got to ride out on the helicopter, and the pilot even let us take a turn at the controls because of our heroics. Well, that's not exactly how it went down.

Brother Campbell was loaded into the helicopter on a stretcher (they brought their own and didn't need to borrow ours). They gave him some better medicine, an oxygen mask, and an IV. He gave us a thumbs-up as they carried him past us, and I felt a lot better about everything.

The rest of the night was a whirlwind. One of the guys in the helicopter stayed with us and gave us some energy bars, hot chocolate from a thermos, and those cool silver blankets that astronauts use. By the time the rest of the search and rescue team got to us, it was almost morning. We had to hike out a different way, since the pathway we took in was still flooded. The Search and Rescue team carried our backpacks, but it was still the most exhausting hike ever.

As we reached the parking lot, I could see a bunch of trucks and an ambulance. Brother Green came running toward us as soon as we came out of the trees. He was crying (hard) and gathered us into a big group hug. "Weak and simple. Yeah right. I've never seen a stronger group of guys. You guys are amazing." Now the rest of us were crying too.

Bishop Christiansen was there with his cell phone, which we each got to use to call our parents.

"Mom? It's Andrew. We're fine. Everyone's fine." She didn't even say anything for thirty seconds. She just cried softly and I'm sure said a prayer.

"I love you, Andrew." That was all she said. That was all she needed to say.

"Tell everyone we'll be home soon. I love you too."

The paramedics checked us out and then told us we could go. I'm not even sure they did all the tests they were supposed to. I think they wanted to get rid of us as quickly as possible. JD had broken one of the windows in the ambulance when he kicked a rock, and Ryan tripped over one of the tables and spilled all of their equipment on the muddy ground. They waved to us as we left, but I'm pretty sure I heard a swear word as I closed the door to the Suburban.

The drive back home took about three hours, and we all slept the whole way. I wasn't expecting much when we got there, probably just Dad and the car to bring me home. I'm sure he had to take some time off work, since it was only Friday. Or was it Thursday? I couldn't even remember.

But the church parking lot was different than I expected. A *lot* different.

There were crowds of people—all of them cheering and waving. The sound was almost deafening as I opened the Suburban door. The crowd collapsed around us, our parents leading the way.

Dad was the first one to me. He pulled me into a big bear hug and said, "Well done, Andy. I'm so proud of you." I guess our story preceded us, because everyone seemed to know what had happened.

Next on the hug list was Paige, who had a few tears in her eyes. Jacob hugged my legs and asked if his pillow was okay. I didn't even know, so I just said yes. Kari was there too, but I knew she would keep her distance. I smelled like moldy campfire, if that's even possible. She smiled and threw her arms around my neck, surprising me and everyone in my family.

"Just make sure you leave your stuff outside." She winked, and I smiled.

Mom was the last one, and she got the longest hug. I've never felt more safe than at that moment.

I looked around the parking lot at the cheering crowd.

The Beehives had made a sign that said, "Welcme Home!" (Yes, it was spelled wrong). Becky was holding the sign and waving at me, and it looked like she had a few tears in her eyes too. But not me. This was my proudest moment.

She made her way across the parking lot and gave

me a high five. "Well done, Andrew." She leaned in and bumped into me on purpose with her shoulder.

"Thanks, Becky. And thanks for your card. It really helped." I bumped her back.

"Anytime." She smiled. "That's quite a scrape you got there."

She touched my forehead with her finger. I had forgotten about that, and I instinctively reached up to feel it too. As I did so, I accidentally touched Becky's hand, and my face felt like it would melt off from all the blushing. I turned away quickly to avoid eye contact.

Ryan was showing the wound on his leg to a small group, including Katie Norton. He was using his hands to demonstrate the size of something—I'm guessing he was describing the porcupine. It looked like he was describing something roughly the size of Doug, though. A little exaggerated, but he deserved it. I wasn't going to rain on *his* proudest moment.

Mason was sitting on the curb, getting a neck rub from his mom. He could have been asleep, but I'm not sure. Curt was drawing a map for his dad, explaining in detail the path we took out of the canyon. JD was eating a hot dog—I have no idea where that came from. Doug was playing a game of hand slap with his older brother.

Laurels smiled and clapped for us. Priests patted us on the shoulders. Parents gave us the thumbs-up sign. Primary kids asked us for autographs. Well, maybe all of that didn't happen, but most of it did.

A car pulled up just as things were winding down. Sister Campbell hopped out and ran to us. She was wearing pajama pants and a BYU T-shirt; it must have been a long night for her. She gave me a hug—one of the tightest hugs I've ever gotten. She went around and hugged each one of us, including Ryland Alcott, a teacher who got mixed up in our group.

"Jeremy—er, Brother Campbell—just got out of surgery. He's going to be okay!" She smiled through her tears. "He told me what you did. You guys are my heroes. Thank you."

Ryland said, "You're welcome" and gave Sister Campbell a hug. Those of us who were *really* on the campout couldn't say much because of the great risk of crying in front of the whole ward. Sister Campbell came around again and gave us each another hug. I didn't make eye contact with any of the other boys, but I could see that we were all blushing pretty bad. Becky caught my gaze and raised her eyebrows. She tried not to smile, but one slipped out into a silent giggle.

After all the tears and hugs, things went back to normal. There wasn't as much media coverage as I had hoped. We were featured in the local newspaper and on a couple of TV news stations, but nothing extensive. The reaction was always the same. The world couldn't believe what we did. Heck, *we* couldn't even believe what we did. But none of that mattered. Heavenly Father knew what we could do, and He helped us do it.

On Sunday, Bishop asked us to get to church early. He didn't have anything special for us to do, but he just asked us to sit in the front row together as a quorum. I don't think I've ever shaken so many hands. Parents, leaders, teachers, kids, and even the stake president came to congratulate us. I felt different. But still the same.

I hadn't grown any stronger. I was still the same kid—weak and simple. I just realized now that I could do a whole lot more than I ever thought I could.

I reached back to fix my collar so the tie wouldn't show.

No luck.

About the Author

Matt Peterson has been working with Scouts and Young Men for over ten years. He has led adventures into deep canyons, up tall mountains, and through raging rivers. Search and Rescue has only been called once.

Matt lives in Mesa, Arizona, with his wife and four kids. He served a mission in São Paulo, Brazil, where he learned Portuguese, how to love the people, and how to walk really fast. In his spare time, he runs a free neighborhood sports league for kids.

0 26575 59995 4